HEARTS IN TURMOIL

Christa Eastwood had first met handsome Hugo Santiago in Gran Canaria, whilst she was distributing leaflets advertising her father's new hotel complex. She had been shocked and angry when Hugo had wrongly accused her of selling timeshare and had put her leaflets in the nearest litter bin. That first meeting didn't bode well for the future, but soon — with a little help from fate — Christa and Hugo found themselves being pushed together more and more . . .

Books by Shirley Allen
in the Linford Romance Library:

SHIRLEY ALLEN

HEARTS IN TURMOIL

Complete and Unabridged

LINFORD
Leicester

First published in Great Britain in 2000

First Linford Edition
published 2002

British Library CIP Data

Allen, Shirley
Hearts in turmoil.—Large print ed.—
Linford romance library
1. Love stories
2. Large type books
I. Title
823.9'14 [F]

ISBN 0–7089–9909–3

Published by
F. A. Thorpe (Publishing)
Anstey, Leicestershire

Set by Words & Graphics Ltd.
Anstey, Leicestershire
Printed and bound in Great Britain by
T. J. International Ltd., Padstow, Cornwall

This book is printed on acid-free paper

1

For what must have been the hundredth time, Crista Eastwood wondered what she was actually doing, standing in a park in Puerto Rico, Gran Canaria, handing out leaflets to tourists who seemed to have descended on the sunny resort in daunting, swarming droves.

Of course, it would please her father, she reflected, grimly.

Crista thought about the train of events which had led to her being here.

From dealing in plush, exclusive, up-market hotels, her father had descended into the boisterous, raucous realms of bulk tourism.

'You've got to move with the times, Cristobel,' he'd remarked, calling Crista by her despised full name, which he occasionally did when he was displeased, or emphasising a point. 'If we want to retain our hold on the business,

1

increase it, in fact, then we've got to be competitive!'

And that was it in a nutshell, she thought, with a trace of bitterness. Her father would never be content with being second best. Yet she was fond of him. They had been on their own for two years now, since her mother was killed in a road accident.

Even if Denise hadn't been killed that fateful morning, there would still only have been the two of them, for she was leaving John Eastwood, her father's company. Crista acknowledged that it must have come as a terrific blow to her father, but she couldn't help but wish that he wasn't so set in his ways, so sure that he was always right! After all, she'd been doing quite well with her art work since leaving college a couple of years previously. A small exhibition of her work in London had led to several commissions, followed by a book of children's stories which she'd written and illustrated herself.

'Art and writing's all very well as a

hobby, Cristobel,' he'd remarked, looking at her disapprovingly, when he'd visited her London apartment just over a week ago. 'But it's a career you should be thinking of, young lady! After all, you're twenty-four now, and I'm not as young as I used to be! I need you in the business with me.'

'But why, Dad? Apart from all the other staff, you've got Stephen, and he knows far more about that sort of thing than I ever will.'

'Stephen,' he'd said carefully, 'like the others, is a paid employee, and that's not the same as family. I want someone at the top whom I can rely on implicitly. And that's you, girl!'

Of course, that wasn't the only reason, Crista reflected now, with a touch of bitterness, as she handed out a leaflet to a middle-aged couple. OK, it might conceivably be the main one, but her relationship with Roger certainly came a close second! Wanting the two men in her life to get to know one another, she'd foolishly arranged a dinner date while her father was in London. It had been a disaster. John Eastwood had taken one look at Roger's ponytail, leather jacket and trousers, and had immediately put him down as a worthless hippy.

All right, so Roger was out of work at the present time, but he did have a first-class honours degree from Cambridge, so something suitable must surely turn up for him soon.

Deep in thought, she didn't even look up as she sensed someone draw near her, simply held out a leaflet.

'Do take one of these,' she said. 'It's an invitation to . . . '

She got no further, as a strong hand clamped over her wrist.

'I'm sick of you human parasites!' the deep menacing voice said. 'You're a disgrace to the country, and if I had my way you'd be locked up.'

Although she wasn't all that sure that she wanted to, she forced her downcast eyes upwards, until they were level with his face. Despite her sudden fear, she had to admit that he was handsome, with dark-lashed grey eyes, at the moment as cold and bleak as a winter's sky. High cheekbones, and a strong jaw line were topped by dark eyebrows, one currently arched derisively. Although at five foot seven, Crista felt as if she was no bigger than a pixie, she looked up at him. She thought he was probably somewhere in his early thirties. Then she became aware that his hard mouth had curved into the hint of a smile, and something in his eyes told her that he was aware of her appraisal, which in turn made her blush like a schoolgirl.

'What? Suddenly rendered speechless? You people aren't normally at a loss for words!'

He surveyed her insolently, his eyes travelling upwards from her sandal-clad feet, long legs, all-too-plainly revealed by her black shorts and figure-hugging white T-shirt. Then his eyes were on her face.

Why on earth had her father decided that she had to learn every aspect of the business, starting at the bottom rung, needless to say, and insisted that she go out distributing leaflets to publicise the opening of his new apartment/hotel set on the cliff side overlooking the bay?

'Well, just what are you going to offer me?' he asked sarcastically. 'A free sightseeing trip, a pack of duty-frees. You're quite a looker, even if your dress sense leaves a lot to be desired! Perhaps if you've something a little more interesting to offer, I might just go along with your little game and visit the Campo Mar or the Marina Verde!'

By this time, his grip on Crista's wrist had loosened considerably. Perhaps she could pull free. She tried, but this obnoxious, arrogant stranger was too quick for her, and his hand fastened round her wrist like a vice.

'Not so fast, sweetheart! Despite that innocent-looking face of yours, I've absolutely no doubt that you've taken many a hapless tourist to the brink of bankruptcy. So why not me? I, at least, can afford it, and I've given you your chance. Come out with me tonight and I'll visit your timeshare resort!'

Timeshare! So he thought she was a timeshare tout! Well, perhaps that partly explained his reaction, but he had no right to be so rude about it. It was on the tip of her tongue to tell him his mistake, when, temper fuelled by his insufferable remarks, Crista thought, why should she? After all, she certainly didn't owe him an explanation!

'You're wasting your time. I wouldn't go out with you if you were the last man on earth! Now, let go of my arm, or I'll call the police. Who are you anyway, that you think you can barge in on me and act exactly as you like?'

'It doesn't matter who I am. Let's just say I don't care for timeshare touts invading my country,' he replied, the slightly bantering note gone from his voice, leaving it icy cold. 'Before I go, I'll relieve you of these.'

Before Crista had time to realise what he meant to do, the stack of leaflets was in his hand, and he was striding purposefully away from her, in the direction of the nearest litter bin, tearing them up as he did so.

Crista was temporarily immobilised, staring after him in wordless fury. How dare he? Why, he wasn't even going to look at them!

'Just a minute!' Crista shouted desperately, as she hurried after him. 'You can't do that!'

'Oh, can't I?' he said softly, as he dropped the remains of the leaflets into the bin and turned sharply on his heel, walking away quickly.

Acting purely on impulse, Crista put her hand into the bin to see if anything was salvageable. Then she drew it out quickly with a sharp gasp of pain as a wasp which she'd disturbed fluttered angrily out of the bin. Crista plunged down on to the nearest bench. Her finger was throbbing unmercifully, and her mind was raging over the despicably rude, arrogant stranger. Who was he? She'd make sure she found out, and make him rue the day he'd riled Crista Eastwood!

There was no sign of John Eastwood at his office in the Margarita Hotel, but his secretary, Gloria, was there when Crista returned.

'What's the matter with you?' Gloria asked, in her barely accented English, as Crista threw herself down in one of the comfortable armchairs, scowling. 'You look as if you have lost every penny.'

'And I feel it, too!' Crista replied, with a wry grimace. 'Where's Dad?'

Gloria, an elegant, sylph-like figure in a red linen dress which suited her dark, exotic colouring to perfection, shrugged slender shoulders.

'Surely you can guess. Senor Eastwood is up at the Argentina!'

Crista ran a hand through her windswept curls. She might have known. Her father was obsessed by his new, purpose-built budget-priced building which was to have its official opening in less than a week's time, although the first guests wouldn't be arriving until about a month afterwards. In Crista's opinion, he was rushing it through. Oh, the façade was impressive enough, with its fountains and myriad of glittering chandeliers adorning the foyer. The reception and restaurant were very chic and stylish, too, as was the ballroom and bar, where the reception she had been handing out tickets for was to be held. Crista couldn't fault the two attractive swimming pools, either, and the gardens were lush and sub-tropical.

But none of these things was the real problem. The rooms and apartments were thrown up in a hurry so that the Argentina could receive its first visitors, and turn in a profit for John Eastwood. But she was being disloyal, Crista told herself, firmly, and probably letting her thoughts run away with her, too. She really must stifle any doubts that tended to tug at her mind when the Argentina was mentioned. Her father was a very successful businessman. He should, no, he must, know what he was doing.

'Has something upset you, Crista?' Gloria asked gently.

'As a matter of fact, it has, in the person of one tall, dark, handsome man with a sarcastic tongue. Do you know him?'

Gloria shook her head, smiling almost wistfully.

'No, but I wish I did! He sounds, how do you say it? Quite a dish!'

'Oh, he's attractive enough visually,' Crista replied, grudgingly. 'But his hateful personality quite nullifies any looks he might have!'

She proceeded to give Gloria an abbreviated, yet graphic account of what had transpired between them in the park. By the time she had finished, two angry splashes of colour were evident in Gloria's cheeks.

'He was very impertinent, this hombre! You should tell your father what happened. I am sure that he would have no wish for his daughter to be spoken to in such a way! I do not know, of course, but from what you have told me, I think that you may have had an encounter with Hugo Santiago. He is a very important man in these parts, and one whom you should, perhaps, be very careful of!'

'But why?' Crista asked, curiously. 'He certainly gave himself plenty of airs and graces, and he definitely seemed extremely objectionable, but why should I have to be careful of him? After all, the likelihood is that I'll never see him again!'

'You'll see him again, Crista, of that I am sure. For one thing, he will wish it! But beware, his nickname is El Diablo, the Devil, and it is one that he didn't get for nothing!'

Crista couldn't help laughing.

'Well, it certainly suits him! He looked quite sinister when he was glowering down at me.'

'It isn't a laughing matter, Crista!' Gloria admonished. 'You're very like Marianne. It's bound to remind him, bring back all that tragedy.'

Before she had a chance to say any more, the telephone shrilled, and she picked it up, speaking in rapid Spanish, so that Crista was unable to make head nor tail of it. Gloria replaced the receiver, and turned to Crista apologetically.

'That was the lawyer's office. I have to take some papers over to them. Could you stay here until I get back? I'll only be about an hour or so.'

'Of course, I'll be happy to! But don't blame me if you get all the wrong messages. You know my Spanish is pretty basic.'

'I'll be as quick as I can, see you!'

Grabbing a large, manila envelope, Gloria was out of the door before Crista could question her further about Hugo Santiago. In the event, she didn't need to. Gloria had been gone less than quarter of an hour, when, with a perfunctory knock at the door, Crista's tormentor from the park strode imperiously into the spacious office. He scowled down at Crista, his lean, handsome face dark and forbidding.

'So, you again,' he said with a shake of his head, the merest hint of a smile curving his lips sardonically. 'I must say, Eastwood continues to surprise me. I wouldn't have expected such an eminent businessman to leave his office in the sole charge of a timeshare parasite!'

Crista got to her feet slowly, face flushed from the man's insufferable rudeness. She drew herself up to her full height and spoke in icy tones.

'I find your remarks, just as I found your previous behaviour in the park, totally offensive! If you've got something to say, would you kindly say it and go about your business. You may have nothing to do all day, but I've got plenty of work to do.'

He looked so angry, that Crista involuntarily took a step backwards, but, to her relieved surprise, he threw back his head and laughed.

'Touché, I suppose I asked for that! Very well, first permit me to introduce myself. I am Hugo Santiago.'

He held out a hand, which, she noticed, was firm and tanned, with long, sensitive fingers. Reluctantly, she took it, and dropped it just as quickly, frightened by the tremor that had passed through her as their hands had clasped. What was the matter with her? She was in love with Roger, and she hated the arrogant man who stood before her.

'And who are you?' he prompted.

'I'm Cristobel E . . . '

No, she wouldn't tell him that she was John Eastwood's daughter. Let him continue to believe that she was a timeshare tout.

'Blencowe,' she finished, using her late mother's maiden name. 'My friends call me Crista.'

'Very well, Cristobel,' he replied, emphasizing the word and leaving Crista unaccountably disappointed.

So he didn't intend to be a friend. Should that really surprise her? Nevertheless, it stung just a little, as he had meant it to.

'I have a message for Eastwood. Will you pass it on to him? Or will you forget, as soon as you go out on one of your little sorties to pressurise our poor, unsuspecting tourists? Come to that, just what are you doing here in Eastwood's office? I know he's stooping low, but surely even he hasn't gone so far down the ladder that he's actually into timeshare now!'

'Do you get some kind of perverted pleasure out of causing pain?' she snapped.

'I'm very sorry,' he said softly. 'I shouldn't have taken my feelings towards Eastwood out on you. It isn't your fault. You're no relation to him!'

Crista's breath caught in her throat. If only he knew! But now was certainly not the time to tell him. Besides which, she needed to find out what he had against her father, and surely Crista Blencowe was far more likely to be able to do that than Crista Eastwood.

'I realise that you're only a time-share tout, but you're only small fry, nonetheless.'

She picked up a note pad, and rushed on quickly.

'But you're getting away from the point Mr Santiago. You said that you had a message for my . . . for Mr Eastwood. If you give it to me, I'll write it down and tell him as soon as possible.'

He smiled derisively.

'Thank you for putting me back in my place, Cristobel! But you still haven't answered my earlier question. Just what are you doing in Eastwood's office? Has he gone into the timeshare business?'

His tone was light, but his expression was anything but. Obviously Crista's answer was important to him, and she wondered why.

'No, of course he hasn't! I'm just standing in for a friend,' she replied, truthfully, surreptitiously looking at her watch as she did so.

Hopefully, Gloria would be back soon. It was just too disturbing being here alone with Hugo Santiago who sometimes looked at her as if he could read her mind as easily as if it were the open pages of a book. He smiled, and it was like the sun suddenly breaking through clouds. Then she scowled. She was being stupid and gullible. Hugo Santiago was arrogant and unfeeling, and she must never lose sight of the fact.

'Good, I'm glad to hear you're not working here,' he replied. 'And now my message. Thank Eastwood for his invitation to the opening of the Argentina. I'll be very pleased to accept. Make sure you tell him that I'll be arriving early. I want to have a good look around the place before the crowds arrive. To get the feel of things, you understand?'

Crista didn't have a chance to answer, for, the next second, he lifted her hand and raised it to his lips. She was so surprised, that the pen and note pad fell from her other hand, her fingers suddenly strangely nerveless.

'Adios, senorita. Hasta la vista. You will make sure that Eastwood gets my message, won't you?'

Crista, in the act of picking up the pen and note pad, nodded. She didn't trust herself to speak!

Gloria arrived back about twenty minutes later, but unfortunately she wasn't alone. Stephen Jacobs, her father's managing director, was with her. Crista had been about to bombard Gloria with questions about Hugo Santiago, and to relay his message for her father, but Stephen's unexpected presence stopped her. Without really being able to say why, she disliked Stephen Jacobs. It was a bit unjust, really, as he was always very polite and gushing to her, perhaps a little bit too much so, with the result that she never felt totally at ease in his company.

'My word, but I am in luck today!' he gushed. 'Not one lovely lady's company, but two!'

'Hi, Stephen,' Crista replied, warily. 'Well, I'm afraid your luck's not going to last that much longer. I'm just on my way.'

She turned to Gloria.

'There were only two phone calls. I've left the messages on that pad.'

'No problems?' Gloria asked, taking in Crista's flushed cheeks.

'None at all,' Crista replied quickly.

There was no way she was going to discuss Hugo Santiago's visit with Stephen standing there all agog.

'I'll probably see you tomorrow, that is, if Dad hasn't got any other plans for me.'

She was heading for the stairs when Stephen caught up with her. Crista paused, surprise dawning in her expressive brown eyes.

'You're not staying in the office then?' she asked.

'I'm going back there, but I wanted a word with you first.' He smiled fulsomely. 'You know, I've been thinking that it must be pretty lonely for you around here, after all, you don't know anyone, and you've only got your dad for company. Well, as you know, I'm pretty well on my own these days, too, since Linda walked out.'

Stephen was separated from his wife, who had custody of their two small children.

'So I thought, well, why don't we help one another and all that? You know there's this nice little bistro, which has recently opened in the new shopping precinct at the top of the Avenida Cornisa. What do you say to going for a meal there tonight?'

Crista gave an involuntary shudder. The last thing she wanted was a date with Stephen Jacobs! Crista thought about saying that she had to wash her hair, then decided that that was too obvious a put-down. After all, she didn't want to antagonise her father's right-hand man at this important stage of his new hotel's development.

'I'm feeling a bit tired, actually, Stephen. Dad's been keeping me pretty busy, and I guess I'm just not used to temperatures of around eighty yet.'

He looked disappointed, and she relented slightly.

'Perhaps some other time! Now, I really must fly. I want to see Dad before he leaves the new hotel. 'Bye!'

She dashed off without a backward glance before he had a chance to answer. As she jumped into her car, she thought what a pity it was that she and Roger hadn't got engaged before she left London. It would have kept creeps like Stephen Jacobs at bay. The difficulty was finance, of course. Crista could well have afforded to buy her own ring, but that didn't seem quite right.

'How long is Dad going to keep me over here?' she murmured to herself, as she tackled the winding road which led down from the hillside into the main town, and then up yet another hill, to where the Argentina was situated.

Of course, he couldn't keep her in Gran Canaria against her will at all, but he'd been a good father in his way, and she didn't want to let him down. Besides, she should really take more interest in what would, after all, be her inheritance. Arriving at the hotel, she parked her car and got out.

The hotel frontage was quite spectacular, with fountains on either side of the main entrance, glistening in the mid-afternoon sunshine. The Argentina sign glittered gold above the revolving glass door. There was no official star-rating as yet, but the tour operators whose reps had visited the property had awarded it a pretty good provisional rating.

She found her father in one of the apartments, berating a Spanish plumber who seemed to be experiencing considerable difficulty in stopping the cold water running. That the bathroom was flooded by two or three inches of water showed Crista that the problem must have been going on for some time.

'Having trouble?' Crista asked, pleasantly, thinking that her father looked quite apoplectic, his heavy face an unflattering red.

He turned round, scowling at her.

'As you can well see!' he barked. 'What are you doing here, anyway? I thought I gave you enough leaflets to keep you out of mischief today.'

'I got through them quicker than expected,' Crista replied, avoiding telling him the truth. 'I think you will have to have the water supply to this apartment turned off, señor. It is going to need some new parts,' the Spanish plumber said.

'I can't do that! All the apartments on this floor are on the same system. If I turn the water off for this one, they all go off.'

The man shrugged.

'There is no other way, Mr Eastwood!'

John Eastwood sighed.

'Very well, see to it!'

He turned back to Crista, brushing his greying dark hair away from his forehead.

'So, to what do I owe the pleasure of this visit? Couldn't Gloria find you a job when you got back to the office?'

'I've been standing in for her while

she went to the lawyers. After that, I was at a loose end, so I thought there might be something I could do here.'

Her father clapped large hands on her shoulders.

'Good girl,' he sighed, looking genuinely pleased. 'I'll go down to reception with you. Luisa can show you how the new computerised bookings system works.'

On their way down, Crista told her father of Hugo Santiago's visit to the office, and of his acceptance of John's invitation to the opening of the Argentina, and what he'd said. John Eastwood stopped in his tracks, staring at her.

'He said what?' he demanded, his face suddenly pale under its suntan.

Crista took the message she'd written down out of her handbag and handed it to him, although she had repeated it to him word perfect.

'Good grief! What the devil is he up to?' John Eastwood exclaimed.

2

Crista went back to the Argentina early the following evening. Following Hugo Santiago's note to her father, she had a distinct feeling that something was wrong, although she didn't know what. Her father had been strangely unforthcoming so she'd decided that the best thing to do was have a thorough look around the place on her own.

To that purpose, she'd deliberately waited until the staff had all gone home, and then obtained the entrance keys from her father's desk. She doubted he'd notice, he was so preoccupied. The keys to the various apartments were easy enough to come by, as they were all in the pigeon holes behind the reception desk.

She decided to have a look around the first-floor apartments to start off with, and hadn't discovered anything more damning than a loose towel rail, a faulty switch and a bed that already had a spring beginning to protrude from it, when she went out on to the balcony of the fourth apartment. It looked directly over one of the large, attractive swimming pools, now filled with water, although the water-heating system wasn't yet in operation.

She stood looking out, hands clasped loosely on the wooden rail. Then she started suddenly. There was a man out there, and he seemed to have binoculars trained on the building. She leaned out farther, trying to recognise him. He was tall and dark, and although she couldn't see his face properly, partly because of the binoculars, nevertheless, if she wasn't mistaken, the intruder was none other than Hugo Santiago!

Crista leaned out still farther, pushing against the wood. Yes, she was positive it was him. But what on earth was he doing here? Spying? Well, it certainly looked very much like it! Mouth set in a grim line, she resolved to go down to the gardens and confront him. Then it happened! One minute she was leaning against the wooden railing, and the next she was spinning through the air, as the railing suddenly gave way.

Terrified, Crista screamed. And then, just as suddenly as she'd fallen, she plunged into the icy waters of the pool, her strapless sandals falling off, and her left foot catching painfully on the concrete surround. Crista, immobilised by shock, went under, coming back painfully to the surface just as Hugo Santiago dived into the water.

Crista found that it was quite excruciating to move her left foot, but she managed to keep herself afloat by moving her arms. The next moment, strong arms closed around her, and she was pulled to the side of the pool.

'Hang on to the side.'

Crista did as he said in silence. Hugo hauled himself out of the pool, then, going down on to one knee, pulled Crista out after him.

'Ouch! Try and be careful!' she cried,

as her injured ankle knocked against the side of the pool.

'What on earth were you doing leaning so far over that balcony? You could have killed yourself!'

Then, without waiting for her indignant reply, he retrieved his binoculars, before sweeping her up into his arms, and striding off with her.

'Where are you taking me?' she asked, her voice hoarse with shock.

Although he was equally wet, somehow, he seemed to be warm. But then, she was probably feeling icy from shock as much as the cold water.

'Into one of the apartments, of course!' he exclaimed, without much patience. 'You've had a nasty shock, and you'll need to get out of those wet things. I suppose Eastwood has seen to it that there's hot running water in the apartments by now.'

'Apart from the second floor,' she replied automatically. 'There was a plumbing problem there yesterday, and the water's still off. The show apartment's probably the best. It's got all the little refreshments, like soap, towels, and, I believe, even towelling robes.'

He looked at her somewhat quizzically. How was a young timeshare tout so knowledgeable about the layout of John Eastwood's building? But now certainly wasn't the time to question her.

'What number is it?' he asked.

'Oh, gosh, the keys!' Crista exclaimed, digging frantically into the pocket of her sodden jeans, and with a little cry of triumph, she fished them out.

'That's it!' Then she looked crestfallen. 'I had another bunch of keys in my pocket as well. They were the ones I was going to look at next before going up to the penthouse. They must have fallen out in the pool!'

'Eastwood can always come along with a fishing net and retrieve them,' Hugo replied as he marched up the steps of the building. 'Did you leave the main door open?'

Crista flushed.

'Yes, I think I did,' she murmured. 'I shouldn't have done, should I?'

'Well, let's say you're very trusting, for a timeshare tout!' he replied, but for once there was no mockery in his voice. 'As it happens, though, it's rather a good thing you did. If you hadn't, it would have meant either breaking in, and I'm sure Eastwood's got a security system, or taking you back to my apartment, which is a couple of miles away, and if you're not going to catch your death of cold, you'll need to get out of those wet things as soon as possible.'

'Not with you there!' Crista was stung into retorting. 'Anyway, you're just as wet as I am.'

'You'll have a hot bath or shower, and then you'll put on one of the bath robes,' Hugo replied, just as if she hadn't spoken. 'As for me, I haven't had a shock, so it won't kill me to go around wet for a little while longer yet. Once I know you can manage on your own, I'll go and fetch some brandy. You'll need it.'

Crista opened her mouth and shut it again, having realised the futility of arguing with him here. She very much doubted that she'd be able to put her left foot on the ground, never mind climb over the side of the bath with it in order to have a shower. But never mind, he'd find out.

'Do the elevators work?' Hugo asked.

'The second one is a bit temperamental, but the other one's OK,' Crista replied, a spasm of pain crossing her face as she did so.

Hugo spotted it, and despite himself, he found that he was suddenly feeling very sorry for her. Without meaning to, he found himself bending his head, and Crista felt the touch of his lips, soft as the caress of a butterfly's wings, against her forehead.

Her eyelids were closing. She was succumbing to sudden violent waves of pain, and her body shook convulsively with reaction to the shock she'd had.

Could she have imagined that delicate kiss, she wondered. It was hard to associate Hugo Santiago with gentleness.

Crista was almost semi-conscious when Hugo unceremoniously sat her down on the bed, and began to unbutton her sodden, pale blue blouse. It was an action which speedily brought Crista back to reality.

'No, you can't do that! I can manage perfectly well myself.'

His eyes showed amusement.

'What a little puritan you are after all! Don't worry, Crista, I'm only trying to help you so that you can have a hot shower.'

'There's absolutely no need, but perhaps you'd be kind enough to help me into the bathroom.'

'OK,' he replied. 'Mind you, I think you're going to have to hop!'

To her dismay, Crista found that he was right. She couldn't get over the side of the bath, either, but, fortunately, the bathroom was fitted with a separate shower cubicle, and she could manage that. Hugo had retired into the other room, having told her to call him when she was ready to come out of the bathroom. It irked Crista that she had to depend on him, but she did, she reflected, ruefully, as the hot jets of water hit her ice-cold skin with stinging force. She dried herself with the large, fluffy bath towel, before slipping into one of the soft robes, tying it tightly around herself.

'All right!' she called.

Hugo came straightaway.

'Better?' he asked, putting his arm about her so that she could lean against him as she made her way back into the lounge.

'Yes, thank you.'

He looked down at her, dark face cynical, as he eased her on to the bed.

'I'm going now to get changed and get some brandy. Don't move while I'm gone. That way you're not likely to get into any more trouble!'

As he strode out of the room, Crista

stared after him angrily. Just who did he think he was, speaking to her just as if she was a delinquent child? And he was in the wrong, when all was said and done! Just what had he been doing training his binoculars on the Argentina, and in the Argentina ground at all, for that matter? Clearly, he was snooping, spying. Quite why, she didn't know, but she had a feeling that her father would be very angry indeed, were she to tell him.

And she was going to, Crista told herself, as she leaned down and examined her throbbing ankle.

'Ouch!' she cried, aloud, as her fingers probed skin that had turned an unbecoming shade of dark purple.

Obviously, she was badly bruised, but was there any deeper damage? Perhaps she would ask Hugo to take a look at it when he returned, for he certainly gave the impression of being the kind of man who would be well up on everything.

She remembered then that she'd left her clothes in the bathroom. If they were going to have any hope of drying, she'd have to put them outside. It was rather doubtful if her jeans would dry, but the other things should, given that it was still quite warm outside. She hobbled off into the bathroom in a somewhat ungainly manner. She picked up the scattered garments and hopped through the room and out on to the balcony. She made sure that she kept well away from the railings, metal in this apartment, and looking a good deal more substantial than the wooden ones in the lower apartment. She spread her clothes out on a couple of plastic chairs. Hopefully, they'd dry, and not blow away.

Just what she was going to wear to go home, and how she was going to get there, was a bit beyond her as she went back into the apartment and settled down on one of the beds. Perhaps Hugo would run her home. Fortunately, she'd defied her father, and insisted on her own apartment for the duration of the time she was in Gran Canaria. After all, wasn't it enough that she'd agreed to move to Puerto Rico and go into the family business? She needed some privacy, some time away from her father.

She sighed. There was no doubt about it, her father was very stubborn. She could never condone her mother's action in leaving them to be with the man with whom she'd fallen in love, but sometimes she felt a sneaking sympathy for her. But, of course, Denise had never managed it. Fate, in the form of a juggernaut, had seen to that as she made that last, fateful journey to Heathrow airport where her lover was to have met her.

Apparently, it had been common knowledge that Denise's frequent, solitary trips abroad were to see her foreign boyfriend. John Eastwood, however, flatly refused to tell Crista any more, despite her cajoling, and her grandmother, Denise's mother, had died when Crista was only ten, and not concerned with knowing the identity of the man with whom her dead mother had fallen in love.

And so it remained a mystery.

Crista's eyelids closed. She supposed that she would have to tell her father that Hugo Santiago had rescued her after her unfortunate accident at the Argentina, but, hopefully, the fact that he might very well have saved her life would go a long way to mitigate the fact of Hugo being in the vicinity in the first place. She didn't want her father to read too much into it, to jump to all sorts of unlikely conclusions. No, much better if she did a little gentle probing herself first.

On that note, she drifted into a pleasant drowsy state. It didn't last long, however. She opened her eyes to a gentle shaking of her shoulder.

'What? Who is it?' she asked, struggling to bring herself back into the land of the living.

'I'm sorry to disturb you,' Hugo said, dryly, 'but you should have this, for the shock.'

He put a glass of brandy into her unprotesting hand as Crista looked up at him dazedly. Hugo was no longer wearing the sodden clothes he'd sported after fishing her out from the pool. Instead, he looked very handsome in a well-fitting cream sports shirt and dark brown trousers. Even his hair looked dry and shining, she thought, a little resentfully, fingering her own damp, tangled hair with her free hand.

'I've been back to my apartment,' he replied, correctly interpreting her thoughts. 'I could hardly go around in soaking wet clothes.'

He put his arm around her shoulders, supporting her.

'Come on now, be a good girl and drink it down, and then you can have something to eat. I've brought you a pizza.'

'A pizza!' Crista exclaimed, gurgling with laughter. 'How very romantic!'

He picked her up on her words immediately.

'So, my little timeshare tout wants a romantic evening, does she? Well, I'll certainly have to see what I can do about that! But not tonight, my pretty one. You'll just have to contain your amorous fervour. After you've had your brandy and eaten your pizza, I'm taking you to the medical centre so that a doctor can check that you haven't broken any bones in your ankle, and then, if they give you the OK, it's back to whatever nefarious lodging you're kipping down in! You'll have to take it easy at the moment. You've had more than enough excitement for one night.'

He looked at her consideringly, his eyes almost hypnotic as they gazed into hers.

'But as to romance, who knows? You're a very attractive lady, and one whom I'd like to get to know very much better.'

As he spoke, he put the glass down on the bedside cabinet, and, before she realised what he meant to do, he sat down on the bed, leaned over her, and

claimed her lips with his own. Crista
had read about magical first kisses, but
dismissed it as fairytale stuff but this
was surely the real thing, the essence
of which daydreams are made. But it
was the wrong thing to do, and some
part of her brain was still capable of
acknowledging the fact. They drew
apart at almost the same time.

'I'm sorry, I shouldn't have done
that,' Hugo said apologetically. 'I
honestly don't know what came over
me. First I tell you you've had
more than enough excitement, and
then I try to add to it! Will you
forgive me?'

Crista nodded. She didn't feel
capable of actual speech.

'Thank you. Right, let's get you to
the table. Your pizza will be cold.'

He sounded so in control whereas
Crista couldn't quite adjust after the
breathtaking unreality of that one kiss.

'What about you? Aren't you going to
eat anything?' she asked, forcing herself
back to reality.

Hugo stood up, and reached out a hand, which Crista took almost reluctantly, annoyed because she could sense her own quivering in his.

'Hurry up,' he said, a suddenly boyish smile spreading over his dark features. 'It's well past meal time, and, yes, I'll be joining you. You've got tomato and cheese, and I've got garlic mushroom. Of course, if you'd prefer to swap, that's no problem at all.'

'No, thanks, cheese and tomato will be fine. Mind you, I'm not sure that I do feel very hungry, more numb than anything else.'

That wasn't quite true. She did feel quite unreal, but she was hardly numb! His kiss had definitely been the most exciting thing that had ever happened to her! But she didn't want to think about it. She couldn't afford to, for even though she wasn't even engaged, she'd always assumed that she and Roger would marry one day.

'Right,' Hugo said, easing her down on to the rather hard kitchen chair, 'I'll just get your pizza, and then you can begin. It's been in the oven for the past twenty minutes or so. When I first got back, you looked so peaceful lying there, that I felt guilty about waking you up.'

'You were here watching me while I was asleep?'

Crista's voice sounded horrified, as Hugo turned from the oven lazily.

'Yes, I quite enjoyed it, as a matter of fact! Anyway, what's so awful in that? I assure you, I've seen other sleeping ladies in my time!'

'Of course, Casanova the Second,' she mumbled.

Hugo looked surprised.

'My dear Crista, if I didn't know better, I'd get the impression that you're jealous! But it's not very likely, is it? You timeshare people don't seem to experience human emotions like others! Instead, you act like mindless, robotic creatures and go out ramping around, tempting innocent tourists.'

'Forget the humbug,' Crista said.

'You said you had a pizza for me.'

It was hurting her inside to be so harsh, yet she knew she had to speak in an uncaring way if he was going to continue to believe the charade which she had imposed on herself. When it came down to it, it was her way of protecting her father. She didn't want Hugo to guess that she was John Eastwood's daughter. She'd better make a pretty good pretence at being a timeshare tout!

'It's gorgeous,' she enthused, gushingly, managing to force down a couple of mouthfuls. 'But so large! I'll never be able to eat it all.'

'And why is that? Dieting? You certainly don't need to,' he said smoothly. 'Your curves are all in the right places!'

Crista spluttered an indignant, 'How dare you!'

Hugo looked amused.

'What an uptight little thing you are! Do tell me, how on earth did someone with your seemingly lofty ideals come to get involved in something so base as timeshare?'

Crista shrugged with a nonchalance she was far from feeling.

'Well, you know how it is, not many jobs around, and the offer of easy money, sun.'

He studied her intently, his eyes boring into hers with searing force so that she found them dropping at the intenseness of his gaze.

'That's exactly what I thought when I met you with those confounded leaflets in the town, but afterwards, well, I wasn't so sure. It seemed to me that there was something more to you, and, believe me, I'm rarely mistaken!'

Crista giggled, in what she hoped was a mindless, irritating way.

'You've got a good opinion of yourself, haven't you?'

Hugo sighed, and, with a sinking feeling of regret, Crista felt unaccountably disappointed when he spoke again.

'Obviously, I was mistaken. Still, I suppose we all make mistakes.'

Then his face broke into an uncharacteristic grin.

'I see that I am not infallible! I suppose the problem is that you're very like someone I once knew.'

His eyes were far away, looking into a distant past.

'But then, didn't she have feet of clay?' he whispered.

It was spoken so quietly, that Crista couldn't be sure whether she'd heard it or not. Curiosity, however, got the better of her. Was this the woman Gloria had mentioned? Mary? Marion? No, Marianne, that was it!

'Who was she?'

Crista leaned forward, eagerly awaiting his answer.

'My wife!' he snapped, harshly, clearly not liking the subject. 'But this conversation isn't getting us anywhere. Eat your pizza, before it gets cold.'

She wanted to question him further, but knew that it would be. She forced herself to eat half of the pizza, then pushed the plate away from her.

'I can't eat any more,' she said. 'But I'll have the brandy now, if you'll get it for me. It's a bit difficult getting up.'

'My pleasure,' he replied, voice neutral, but she knew he was angry, and she felt sure it was because he was still thinking about his wife.

Obviously, they were no longer together, and she longed to know what had happened. Clearly, whatever it was, Hugo considered it to be his ex-wife's fault. As Crista took the glass, their fingers brushed, and she drew back as if she'd been scorched by a flame. Although he was objectionable, there was no doubt that Hugo Santiago was a force to be reckoned with. The sheer power of the man was quite frightening, as was her unwilling attraction to him.

'Come and sit on the settee. You'll be more comfortable,' he said, in a much gentler tone, having noticed the look of pain which had crossed Crista's delicate features. 'Here, I'll help you.'

She climbed unsteadily to her feet, or, in this instance, foot, the other one still having to be held in the air, and Hugo helped her over to the sofa, easing her down on to it. Then he handed her the still half-full brandy, and went over to one of the cupboards and poured himself a measure.

'Should you be drinking if you are driving me to the medical centre?'

His firm lips curled derisively.

'I assure you, Cristobel, that I'm not one of the lager louts which your country seems to be producing in ever-increasing numbers!'

Crista baulked at his arrogant words.

'Indeed not,' she replied sarcastically. 'No one could possibly mistake such a fine Spanish gentleman for anything so common!'

'I'm only half-Spanish,' he replied, in what, for him, seemed an almost defensive tone. 'My mother was as English as you are.'

Despite her efforts to not show it, Crista was intrigued.

'I suppose that explains why you're called Hugo, after all, it's not a Spanish name is it? Where in England did your mother come from?'

'Cornwall,' he said, his face closed and shuttered. 'Anyway, it's time we were going to the medical centre.'

'Right,' Crista replied, irritated. 'Although I would have thought that you'd have at least checked on my ankle yourself, otherwise we may look very stupid when we get there!'

He looked at her coldly.

'Why should I? I rescued you, but why should I feel any further obligation?'

Crista looked at him with loathing.

'For your information, I could have got out of that swimming pool myself!' she cried, untruthfully. 'Come to that, what were you doing snooping around the grounds of my father's . . . '

She broke off abruptly, her hand clamping her mouth. Oh, no! What had she done! He'd made her so angry that she'd revealed who she was!

3

Hugo walked across the floor casually. Crista could never be quite sure afterwards, but she thought he'd even had his hands in his pockets. His voice was full of mocking as he spoke.

'So, my dear little timeshare tout, you want to know what I was doing in your father's . . . and then you realised just what you'd said! Right, Cristobel Eastwood, just why did you lie to me?'

'I didn't do it deliberately,' Crista replied, in a voice that wasn't quite steady. 'It was your mistake in the first place! You were very rude to me when I met you in the park. You wouldn't listen to anything I tried to say, in fact you made no effort at all to understand!'

'And just, precisely, what was I supposed to understand?'

'That I was distributing leaflets for the opening of the Argentina. You assumed that I was a timeshare tout, but I didn't say so!'

'Very well,' he agreed, reluctantly, 'I'll grant you that. But you hardly bothered to contradict me now, did you?'

Crista faced him unflinchingly.

'You hardly gave me a chance! You were so puffed up with your own importance, that you just weren't prepared to listen to anything which a poor, unsavoury mortal like myself had to say.'

'No one speaks to me like that,' he began, his face hard.

'And lives!' Crista interrupted, goaded beyond endurance.

To her surprise, Hugo threw back his head and laughed.

'You've got one thing going for you, Cristobel Eastwood,' he said, with grudging admiration. 'You've certainly got spirit.'

Crista smiled weakly, suddenly feeling an overwhelming surge of tiredness sweep through her body.

'Do you mind if we leave all this for

now? Today's been very stressful, and I just feel as if I want to go home.'

'And where is that? The Margarita Hotel?'

'No. I have an apartment, a private one.'

'I wonder why,' he mused, not waiting for, or expecting, an answer. 'Right, but before I take you there, you're going off to the medical centre.'

'But how can I go there?' Crista asked. 'My clothes aren't going to be dry yet.'

'I'd already thought of that,' he replied. 'I'll help you into the bathroom where you'll find some things which I think should fit you. They belonged to my wife, Marianne, and if appearances are anything to go by, they should fit you perfectly. You resemble her a great deal.

By the tone of his voice, that certainly wasn't a compliment! Obviously, Hugo felt very bitter towards his wife. And she was called Marianne. So Gloria had seen the resemblance between Crista and Hugo's wife, too. Was he still with her? Were they divorced? There were so many things that Crista wanted to ask him, needed to know.

'You brought her clothes here?' she said at length, not quite able to keep the resentment out of her voice.

'Considerate of me really, wouldn't you agree? After all, as you said yourself, your clothes won't be dry yet, and you've got to wear something.'

'But doesn't she mind?'

'I hardly think so! You see, my wife and I are divorced. To the best of my knowledge, she's living in Sweden.'

His voice was cold, and his expression forbidding. Clearly, that was all he was prepared to say.

'It was kind of you to bring them,' Crista ground out, and after he'd helped her into the bathroom, she closed the door firmly behind her, looking speculatively at the clothes which had belonged to his wife.

There was cream satin underwear, and a short, turquoise silk designer dress. It was a deceptively simple smock, and clearly very expensive. It suited her colouring very well, and, as with the other garments, could have been made for her. But it was a strange feeling to wear his ex-wife's clothes, although it was a thoughtful gesture on Hugo's behalf.

His eyes darkened perceptively as Crista emerged from the bathroom, hanging on to the door for support.

'You look beautiful,' he said, simply, his face a tight mask of pain. 'I should have realised that John Eastwood would be my justice! Come on, the sooner I get you to the medical centre the better!'

The following day, Crista was virtually housebound. The doctor who had examined her at the medical centre had been adamant that she would have to rest for a few days. Although she hadn't broken any bones, her ankle was very badly bruised, and had become quite swollen.

At least the weather was gorgeous, so

she would be able to sit out on her balcony, as long as she rested her foot on a stool. She'd felt duty-bound to ring her father and tell him what had happened. This had led to complications, however, as it forced her to reveal that Hugo had been in the Argentina grounds. Her father's reaction startled her. She'd expected him to be angry, but not quite so incensed.

'Good grief, girl, what on earth are you thinking about?' he'd roared into the phone. 'All this happened last night and you've only seen fit to tell me now! Do you realise it's gone ten o'clock? By now it's likely to be spread over the local papers that the Argentina's unsafe! At that rate, we may not be able to fulfil our booking obligations. By the saints, I could be ruined because of you and Santiago!'

Not a word about her injury. No thought for the fact that she could have been killed, Crista thought, with increasing resentment.

'I'll have to see to this straight away,'

he went on. I'll be in touch with you later!' he exclaimed and then he'd hung up.

Crista laboriously made herself some toast and coffee, inwardly berating her father as she did so. Surely he should have offered to send someone over to help her, or, at the very least, enquired if she needed any assistance. But it wasn't in her nature to feel self-pity for long, and once she'd breakfasted, and gone out on to the balcony, she began to wonder just why her father had been so upset.

Was it possible that her father and Hugo were somehow in competition against one another? The more she thought about it, the more sense it seemed to make. Hugo had clearly been spying the previous evening. Oh, and hadn't she helped him to see the place! She grimaced, thinking what a fool he must think her. She'd played right into his hands.

She had to speak to Gloria, get her father's secretary to tell her all she

knew about Hugo Santiago. Cursing
her injured ankle, Crista hobbled
painfully back into the apartment, and
dialled the number of the Margarita
office. Gloria answered rightaway.

'Gloria, it's Crista. Tell me, what
exactly does Hugo Santiago do for a
living?' she asked, without preamble.

Gloria's laugh tinkled down the
phone.

'Hugo Santiago? Don't tell me that
you're interested in him, Crista? Oh, I
know he's a very attractive man, but
he's a dangerous one, too, and someone
your father most definitely wouldn't
approve of.'

Crista gave an impatient sigh. She
should have guessed that Gloria would
think that she was interested in Hugo,
and she wasn't! She just had to get to
the bottom of the mystery surrounding
him, and Gloria, having worked for
John Eastwood for several years, was
the best person to help her.

'I'm curious about him, that's all,'
she replied, and then gave Gloria an

abbreviated version of what had happened the night before.

Gloria was immediately all concern.

'Oh, poor Crista! You must be feeling really uncomfortable! I'm on my own here, but Stephen should be in later, so I can come over and help you.'

'Thanks, Gloria, but really, there's no need. I'm just going to take things easy for a day or two. No, just tell me what you know about Hugo. All of it.'

'OK, if that's what you want, although I do not know how much your father would want you to hear.'

'Gloria, I'm an adult!' Crista exploded. 'My father doesn't come into it.'

'Very well. I understand that your father and Hugo's father were once business partners, but they had a disagreement, went their separate ways.'

'What was the disagreement about?'

'It was before my time, but I did hear that there was a woman involved. I do not know the exact details. Anyway, nowadays, they are bitter enemies businesswise, particularly as Hugo's company has been doing so well. You see, after Hugo's tragedy, he became a bit ruthless, a tough businessman.'

'But what was Hugo's tragedy? Was it to do with his wife?'

'In part. He was married to a woman called Marianne. A very beautiful woman, in fact, a lot like you, physically. Mentally, she was a social butterfly, the kind of woman a man is proud to be seen with, but who shirks responsibility and is totally incapable of being a responsible mother. She left Hugo and returned to her native Sweden with their little son. I think the boy's name was Robin. Anyway, Hugo was frantic. The child meant everything to him. He would have got custody, I am sure, but before he was able to, Robin died. He had fallen down the stairs while his mother was out. The rumour was that she was partying with her new boyfriend.'

'Oh, how terrible!' Crista exclaimed. 'And I remind him of her.'

She began to understand Hugo's antagonism towards her. There was a double tragedy. One in the past which Gloria only knew sketchily and another more recent one, one which must be a raw, open wound for Hugo, a wound which would fester every time he set eyes on her.

'Were the police involved?' Crista asked.

'I think so, I don't really know. As I said, it was in Sweden. We only really knew here what we read in the newspapers, but there was quite a bit because Hugo Santiago was a prominent man. I think they referred to him as the most prominent hotelier in the Canary Islands at that time.'

'Thank you for telling me that, Gloria, you've clarified things quite a lot,' she said with a sinking feeling in her heart.

'Not at all, although I hope I've done the right thing in saying what I have. You are sure that you don't want me to come over? It is no trouble.'

'Thanks, Gloria, but I'm managing fine. I'll see you when I'm more mobile. Thanks again.'

As she replaced the receiver, she was disturbed to find that her hand was trembling. She still didn't know just why Hugo Santiago had been in the Argentina grounds — probably he had been spying. But she couldn't find it in her heart to think too badly of him, at least not for the moment. Crista was still thinking about Hugo when the intercom shrilled.

'Crista Eastwood speaking.'

'Hugo Santiago.'

The deep voice sent an unwelcome tremor down her spine.

'I need to talk to you. May I come up?'

'Yes, yes, of course!' Crista replied, feeling completely stunned.

But she didn't get long to think about his sudden, unexpected arrival, for a few moments later her doorbell rang and she opened the door to find him standing there.

'How are you?' he asked, his expression strangely tender. 'You know, I've been quite worried about you. You shouldn't be on your own.'

Crista was disconcerted. Whatever she'd been expecting, it certainly wasn't this gentle approach! Nervously, she passed a hand through her hair.

'I'm a lot better, thank you. But do come in.'

As he followed her into the room, she sank down on to the sofa. She indicated a chair opposite. At least then she wouldn't be at such a distinct disadvantage. He was so tall that he tended to overshadow the room.

'I would have thought that your father would have been here. Or at least sent one of his minions to help his only child!'

So would I, Crista almost said but then decided that it sounded disloyal. Besides, there was something she must pick him up on.

'How did you know I was an only child?'

Hugo sighed, then his handsome face broke into a smile.

'I see I've given myself away! I know because my father and yours used to be business partners.'

So Gloria had been right. Well, here was her chance to find out something more about the link between Hugo and her father, and to hopefully solve the mystery of why they were now at loggerheads.

'Used to be? But what happened? Did they fall out?'

'Yes, they had quite a severe disagreement and your father bought mine out of the business.'

'What was it all about?' she persisted.

'You don't know anything?' he said. 'Your father never told you?'

Crista shook her head.

'He's still bitter about it,' he said, more to himself than to her.

'About what?' Crista asked. 'What did happen?'

'All right, I think you have the right to know, and it's all water under the bridge now. Your mother fell in love with another man. She was going to leave your father for him.'

'Yes, yes, I know that much,' Crista interrupted, her eyes alight with excitement. 'But I've never known who. No one would ever tell me.'

'I'll tell you,' Hugo replied, his voice expressionless. 'It was my father.'

Crista looked at him, speechless.

'And that's why there's no love lost between you and my father!' she exclaimed. 'Oh, now I understand!'

'Oh, do you? Sweet, innocent little Crista, I wonder if you really do! But I didn't come here to talk about the past. I came to see if I can be of any help to you. Have you had anything to eat? Vico's restaurant does very good lunches, and I'd be only too happy to take you there.'

She gave a nervous laugh, and Hugo looked quite hurt.

'Are my overtures at friendship so comical?' he asked.

'Not at all!' Crista replied, with a smile.

Then she looked down at herself ruefully, realising for the first time that she was wearing only a swimsuit, with a robe pulled on hastily after the intercom had shrilled.

'But everything's so awkward due to my ankle! I look a sight!'

'Actually, you look quite beautiful, but then you always do,' he replied, gallantly, although his face was surprisingly grim, and Crista couldn't help but wonder if he was thinking of his wife, whom she resembled.

Aloud, she said, 'Thank you, but it's not true! Still, if you'll bear with me, I'll do my best to make myself at least presentable.'

'Take your time. I'm giving myself a day off today, so there's no hurry.'

Crista showered, and then changed into a cool, crisp, lemon cotton dress. It had been relatively inexpensive, but it was still one of her favourites. She'd managed quite well and was feeling pleased with herself when she went back into the lounge.

Her new-found calmness didn't last long, as she saw that Hugo was sitting reading the notes for a story she was working on when she could and looking at the illustrations intently. Seeing him, all the questions Crista had planned to ask him went flying out of her head like lost daydreams.

'What on earth do you think you're doing!' she cried angrily, trying to hurry towards him, planning to pull the file out of his hands.

It didn't work. Instead, her injured ankle gave way under her and she landed in an undignified heap at his feet. Hugo put the file down slowly, then gazed down at her, his expression mocking.

'Tut, tut! See what temper does for you! Now I wonder just how you intend to get up.'

'You're going to help me, of course!'

'Am I?' he asked. 'And why do you think I should do that?'

'Don't play games with me!' Crista cried desperately, knowing that she couldn't manage to get up on her own.

'Who said I'm playing games?' he returned.

'All right, please help me up, you arrogant devil!'

Hugo eyed her considerably.

'Not very graciously put, but still, I'm not an unfeeling man.'

He picked her up and deposited her on the settee. Crista struggled up into a sitting position, her face tight with fury, her previous sympathy for him completely forgotten in the face of his unyielding arrogance.

'Do you get some perverse kind of kick out of making me suffer?' she demanded.

'Obviously so, my dear!' he agreed cheerfully. 'Didn't you tell me I was some kind of pervert when we had our little encounter in the park?'

'Devil!' Crista muttered.

'I beg your pardon?'

'I said devil! That's what your name means, isn't it? And very well merited, even if you did have a hard time!'

Then she had the grace to blush.

'Oh, I'm sorry! I didn't mean to rake up the past.'

Her voice trailed off lamely and Hugo picked her up on it, his eyes narrowed.

'How do you know about that?' he demanded. 'And what do you mean by saying you're sorry?'

Crista gulped. He looked so angry all of a sudden. But she couldn't see any way out of it, she'd just have to explain.

'Gloria told me about your little boy, about what happened to him, so I can understand why you feel bitter and why . . .'

Hugo's face was a dark mask of pain.

'She had no right to, damned, interfering woman! Just what else has she said about me?'

'She didn't want to tell me anything, actually. But I insisted that she did.'

He still looked annoyed but a little of the tension had left his face.

'Oh, and why? Are you just a natural

busybody or do you have some deeper interest in me?'

By this time, he was sitting on the settee beside her, his handsome face disturbingly close to her own. Uncomfortably aware of the erratic beating of her heart, Crista drew away.

'You'd mentioned that I resemble your ex-wife and so had Gloria. I found the thought disturbing and I wanted to know more about her.'

'I see. So you want to talk about Marianne. I can't say I find the subject pleasing but if you want to, then we will. But first, let's go out for lunch.'

'All right. If you want to take me out for lunch, then I'll come.'

Vico's was a small, intimate restaurant in the attractive yachting port of Mogan. Crista hadn't yet managed a trip there, although it was only about quarter of an hour's drive from Puerto Rico. She immediately fell in love with the narrow, flower-lined streets, the attractive eighteenth-century-style balconied houses and the quaint harbour with its profusion of yachts.

'It's gorgeous!' she exclaimed, her mind temporarily distracted from thoughts of Marianne Santiago and Hugo's promise to talk about her.

Hugo looked at her lovely, heart-shaped face, suddenly sparkling with happiness and his heart gave a foolish leap. Surely he wasn't falling in love with John Eastwood's daughter — Crista, who had a startling resemblance to his selfish, irresponsible ex-wife. He grimaced. After what Marianne had done, he had no wish to fall in love with anyone at all and relationships between himself and Eastwood were, to put it mildly, strained, and likely to get worse in view of his suspicions about the Argentina's safety.

Crista was leaning heavily on his arm. She was walking quite well, really, but he saw a sudden spasm of pain cross her face and quickly led her into the restaurant.

'Thanks,' she murmured, gratefully. 'I'd like to walk around but I'm afraid I'm not really up to it. Still, it's nice to get out. I hate just sitting around at home not doing anything.'

Even as she spoke, the words struck her as comical, and she laughed softly. Home! What about the flat in London? What about Roger? Could she really think of Puerto Rico as home in such a short time?

'What were you laughing at?' Hugo enquired as they were shown to the best table in the place.

Clearly, Hugo was a known and respected figure at Vico's.

'Just the fact that I said home. I've only been in Gran Canaria a week. It seems strange that I should have thought of it as home so quickly.'

'Where were you before?' Hugo enquired as they were handed menus.

'In London. I went to art college there and I just stayed on.'

'Any luck with the art?' he asked, his gaze serious. 'You're very good, you know, both your writing and your artwork. I don't know why you didn't want me to look at it!'

To her chagrin, Crista blushed.

'We arty types are a sensitive lot,' she replied lightly. 'Anyway, it's still only in its infant stages and the way it's going on, I might very well scrap the whole thing yet! I know Roger didn't think much of it.'

Now why had she said that? She certainly had no wish to discuss Roger with Hugo Santiago!

'And is this Roger qualified to make such a statement?' he asked.

'Roger's brilliant,' she replied. 'But, no, he's no authority on art, nor children's stories! They're beneath his dignity! Roger's a historian, and a very good one. I don't doubt he'd be able to tell you the exact moment Henry the Eighth decided to have Anne Boleyn's head chopped off!'

'How very morbid! Does Roger have some kind of fascination with violent death?' he asked, face expressionless.

'I only meant it as an example,' Crista replied quickly.

She turned her attention back to her

menu, which was safer than dwelling on Roger's attributes or lack of them. They decided on seafood cocktails, followed by salad, accompanied by a bottle of white wine.

'Who is this Roger, by the way?' Hugo enquired as they finished their cocktails.

'My boyfriend,' Crista mumbled, hoping that he wasn't going to pursue the subject.

'I see. Serious?'

'I thought so but now I don't know,' she replied, and then realised that she must have given him quite the wrong impression altogether! 'My father certainly doesn't like him.'

Hugo's face tightened.

'That doesn't really surprise me. I would imagine Eastwood's the possessive type. Yet, somehow, I would also think that they'd find your Roger somewhat preferable to me!'

Crista was saved from answering that by the arrival of their main course.

They ate their meal in comparative

silence, Crista's mind dwelling unhappily on her father and about what he'd said on the phone. She should be here questioning Hugo over his spying activities at the Argentina, yet instead, she'd succeeded in giving him the impression that she was no longer sure how she felt about Roger now that she'd met him! And what of Marianne? Hugo had said that they'd discuss her, and yet they hadn't.

Crista pushed her plate away from her, wiping her hands on the napkin.

'That was very nice. I gather that you're in the same line of business as my father. Was Marianne involved, too?'

'More of Gloria's little confidences, I gather? I'll answer the second part of your question first. Marianne took very little interest in the business. In fact, she took very little interest in anything other than clothes and parties! But Marianne can come later, if she has to. Personally, I would prefer to forget that the undoubtedly beautiful, but utterly shallow, woman ever existed! Yes, I'm in the same type of business as your father. You've heard of Voyager Travel, I expect?'

Crista nodded. It was a household name. Originally a company which specialised in holidays for the mega-rich, it had widened its horizons and brought quality holidays into the reach of the general public. In short, it was the success story of the decade. But she hadn't known that Hugo Santiago was the man behind it. One thing she did know for certain, though — her father had known. And he was fiendishly jealous of Voyager Travel. In fact, she'd been brought up to believe that Voyager Travel wasn't what it was made out to be, wasn't to be trusted at all.

'That means that you're my father's main rival and his enemy,' Crista said miserably, for her loyalties should surely lie with her father.

'Not from my choice,' Hugo replied, and she saw that his expressive eyes were dark with emotion. 'I've suggested to Eastwood several times that we amalgamate again but he remains implacable!'

'Yes, he would. He's a very stubborn man,' Crista had to agree. 'But that doesn't give you the right to snoop around his property.'

'I will do anything in my power to prevent that place opening! Surely even you must realise that it isn't safe! Look what happened to you. If you'd fallen on to the concrete instead of into the pool, you'd have been killed!'

'You mean that you intend to sabotage my father's plans?' she cried, her voice suddenly shrill. 'The Argentina is his whole life right now. It would destroy him for something like that to happen.'

Then she became aware that the waiter was once more at their side.

'You would like a dessert, perhaps, or coffee?' he asked.

'Only coffee, please,' Hugo replied, curtly.

'You're going to ruin him, aren't you?' Crista continued. 'He said you'd planned it all, that by now it would be in the papers!'

Tears stung at her eyes, making them glisten.

'I can't believe how stupid and gullible I've been.'

'We can't discuss it here,' Hugo replied. 'Excuse me a moment.'

And before Crista had a chance to utter any protest, he went to the cash desk and settled the bill.

'Come on!' he said, his face inscrutable, as he unceremoniously grasped hold of her arm and pulled her to her feet.

'There's no need to hold on to me like that!' she protested as he frog-marched her out of the restaurant.

He ignored her protest completely, just pulled her along the short distance to where his black Mercedes was parked.

'How dare you!' Crista cried, twisting in his grasp, but, to her fury, making little impact. 'How much more harm do you mean to inflict on my father?

Hasn't your family done more than enough to him?'

She was beside herself with rage, her ankle throbbing painfully, her brain a clouded jumble of emotions.

'You planned it all, didn't you?' she raged at him. 'You paid a photographer to be at the Argentina last night so that he could capture my fall on film, and then you could give the papers photos to back up your story that the Argentina isn't safe! You're despicable! Well, say something for goodness' sake!'

Only when they were both in the car, and speeding towards Crista's apartment, did he actually deign to speak.

'How typically Eastwood,' he said, his voice chilling as he looked at her with angry contempt. 'To condemn without the benefit of a trial! For your information, Miss Eastwood, it would have been quite impossible for me to have engaged a photographer to capture your inglorious demise into the swimming pool! How could I? How did I know you were going to even be there, let alone conveniently fall off the balcony!'

'Oh, that's simple enough!' she retorted. 'You followed me, saw me going into the Argentina and then you and your photographer friend wandered around spying, hoping to catch something incriminating on film!'

She was looking away from him as she spoke, her eyes suddenly alighting on a newsagent's placard. The headline screamed at her.

Argentina peligrosa.

Dangerous! Even her limited Spanish told her that! Her eyes fixed on him, burning with temper.

'Look at that! It's in the papers already! Oh, I'll never forgive you for this!'

'What do you mean?' he countered.

'Don't pretend you don't know! It was there, on the placard!'

'I'm driving a car, not on a sightseeing tour. What was on the placard?'

'That the Argentina's dangerous, of

course! And it's all your fault!'

'Cristobel, be quiet! This is a very busy stretch of road, and there's no way that I can concentrate on driving and carry on an argument with you.'

She didn't trust herself to speak. Hugo Santiago was obviously guilty and she'd trusted him, to the extent of betraying her father.

The journey back to her apartment seemed endless, although Hugo was driving as fast as he safely could, presumably anxious to get rid of her as soon as possible and continue his campaign of terror against the Argentina, she thought, angrily. That she herself had had doubts about the building's safety came unwillingly to her mind, but she brushed the thought away. Experienced as he was in the travel business, her father would surely be aware of the shortcomings, wouldn't he?

She must not let herself weaken now. Hugo had shown himself to be a hard, unscrupulous man. That he had become that way due to his wife's betrayal and his young son's death was tragic, but she couldn't allow it to cloud her judgement, couldn't allow herself to be disloyal to her father. Yet she felt unreasonably depressed at the prospect of being on the opposing side to Hugo. As they finally drove into Puerto Rico, Crista dared to steal a glance at him. His profile was cold and withdrawn. He felt her eyes on him and glanced at her. She coloured slightly and looked away.

What a mess, Hugo thought harshly. If only Eastwood wasn't such a self-opinionated man, harbouring grudges that should have been allowed to die a natural death years ago. After all, he could feel bitter, too. It was his mother who had been betrayed! After Denise Eastwood's death, Ramon Santiago had seemed to lose all zest for living and it was rumoured that his yachting acci-dent, several months after Denise's death, in which he'd lost his own life, hadn't in fact been an accident at all, but suicide. The verdict had been accidental death but it hadn't stopped the rumours.

His mother, sweet, gentle Claire, never in good health, had been particularly wounded by all the malicious gossip which was why they'd moved from the family home in Tenerife to neighbouring Gran Canaria. Yet it had all been in vain and Claire had died less than eighteen months after Crista's mother's fateful car crash. Hugo, twenty years old at the time, and studying for a degree at London University, had dropped out to found Voyager Travel with the help of his elder sister, Elena, who had since married an American and was now living in Texas.

In the early stages, he, too, had felt bitterness but then he'd come to realise that he and John Eastwood were only injured parties and that there was absolutely no sense in them remaining at loggerheads, when, through amalgamation, they could easily make themselves one of the world's foremost tour operators. He had tried on several occasions to make Eastwood see the wisdom of this but the older man had remained implacable, although, of recent times, his antagonism had become slightly less obvious, hidden, as it was, under a fine veneer of politeness.

This explained why he'd been invited to the Argentina's official opening, as one of the multitude who would undoubtedly be there, seeing what John Eastwood wanted them to see, and not what was actually going on behind the scenes. He pulled into the small carpark which was at the back of Crista's apartment block, his mind churning. He'd have to expose what Eastwood was doing. There was no avoiding it unless the older man could be per-suaded to see reason. But he doubted it. And the problem was that Crista was going to be caught up in it all and the last thing he wanted to do was hurt her.

He caught his lip between his teeth, thinking how harsh, arrogant, and thoroughly unreasonably he'd acted towards her on their first encounter in the park. Seeing her standing there had brought back memories of Marianne, and far, far worse, of Robin, the son he'd lost.

Then again he'd also thought that Crista was a timeshare tout and he hated those people with almost religious fervour. Crista could have put him straight but she hadn't, had she? No, she'd probably been too busy laughing at his expense. And here he was feeling sorry for her!

He laughed silently. Just what sort of a fool was he? Hadn't he suffered enough at Marianne's hands?

'Come on!' he said, rather harshly. 'I'll help you up to your apartment.'

He reached across her and opened the passenger door.

'I don't want you to feel you have to help me,' she began.

'My pleasure!'

But he looked as if it was anything but, as he got out of the car and went round to her side, and helped her up. Crista's ankle had stiffened during the car journey and she stumbled and would have fallen, only for Hugo's arms coming quickly around her, momentarily clasping her to him. Crista felt a tremor quiver through her body, and could have sworn that there was an answering tremor in his, before he thrust her from him almost savagely, although he was careful to keep a tight grip on her arm to steady her.

The only elevator wasn't working.

'Oh, no!' Crista exclaimed. 'This would have to happen today!'

'It's not such a tragedy,' he replied calmly.

Then, before she had any idea of what he was going to do, he'd swept her up into his arms, and was striding out for the staircase. Almost carried over the threshold, Crista thought to herself, with a slightly hysterical giggle.

'You find it amusing?' he enquired, looking down at her.

'Not at all!' Crista replied truthfully.

She wasn't in the slightest bit amused. Stressed and strained, yes, and miserable at the prospect of only ever seeing him again as an enemy.

When they got to the top of the stairs, Hugo carried her along the corridor where her apartment was the last one on her right.

'It's all right, I can manage on the flat,' Crista exclaimed.

'Keep still,' he commanded, face set. 'We're almost there.'

'No, it can't be.'

Crista's exclamation was horror-stricken as her father came to the door of the apartment, looked down the corridor, and saw her in Hugo's arms. A look of dismay glazed John Eastwood's features. Then, with a bellow of rage, he advanced towards them.

'How dare you, Santiago!' he shouted. 'Your father stole my wife, now you're trying to do the same with my daughter! Isn't my hotel enough for you? Splattered in all the papers, thanks to you! Put her down, damn you.'

Hugo, his lean, dark face totally inscrutable, gently put Crista down, one arm still supporting her. John advanced with his fists clenched up at Hugo.

'Aren't you a bit old for these childish games, Eastwood?' he asked mockingly, a muscle at the side of his mouth moving ever so slightly.

John Eastwood's face was puce, his breathing suddenly laboured, as he swung a clumsy punch in Hugo's direction, missed, lost his balance on the marble floor surface, and fell heavily.

'Oh, no! Dad!' Crista cried, dashing to his side.

She kneeled down, her hand on his forehead. It was moist and clammy. She looked up at Hugo accusingly.

'You've killed him!'

4

The next moment, Hugo was beside her, his hand feeling for John Eastwood's pulse. It was faint, but unmistakably there.

'He's not dead, Crista,' he said, gently. 'But I think he may have suffered a heart attack. If you give me the key to your apartment, I'll go and phone for an ambulance. You stay with him.'

Crista looked at Hugo with large, frightened eyes.

'He will be all right?'

'I'm sure he will,' Hugo murmured soothingly. 'But it's important to get help, so give me your key, Crista.'

Crista handed over the key, and then turned her attention back to her father. She put her arm behind his head, raising it slightly.

'Oh, Hugo, hurry up!' she implored the empty corridor.

Her frantic thoughts were suddenly interrupted by Hugo's return, as he kneeled down beside her.

'You've got through to them?' she asked urgently.

'Yes, don't worry, Crista, they're coming straight away. You look very tired, Crista. Why don't you go and sit in the apartment? I'll wait here until the ambulance men come.'

'No! He's my father. And I'm staying with him! After all, surely even you can see that I've already caused him enough harm.'

'It wasn't your fault, Crista. It was probably unfortunately timed, but we couldn't know that he was going to be here and would jump to all the wrong conclusions, now could we?'

'It is my fault. I shouldn't have agreed to go out with you in the first place. After all, you're his enemy, you're working against him.'

Hugo's arm was suddenly round her shoulders, and he was drawing her into an embrace.

'I don't want to be his enemy, Crista,' he said, his breath warm against her face. 'And I most certainly don't want to be yours.'

Crista pulled away from him, her eyes dark with temper.

'How dare you make overtures towards me when my father's lying here so ill? Haven't you got any sense of decency at all?'

'Crista, try and keep calm. I was only trying to comfort you.'

'I don't need your type of comfort. In fact, I don't need you here at all.'

'Nevertheless, you've got me here, and I'm staying,' he replied grimly.

Crista made no answer, because at that moment two men carrying a stretcher were hurrying along the corridor towards them. They spoke to Hugo in rapid Spanish.

'What are they saying?' she demanded of Hugo, as the men put John Eastwood on the stretcher and turned to go.

'They just asked what happened, that's all. Come on, we can go with him to the hospital.'

'You don't need to come.'

'Oh, no? Cristobel, I think I do! After all, if I don't accompany you, what are you going to do for an interpreter?'

Fortunately, the hospital of Nuestra Senora was only a five minutes' drive away. Crista and Hugo were shown into a waiting area, while John Eastwood was taken into the Intensive Care Unit. Hugo made several attempts at conversation, but Crista replied in curt monosyllables, so that he subsided into silence, guessing that she was too shocked to want to talk.

After several minutes, which to Crista felt more like hours, she asked, 'How long are they likely to be?'

'Quite a while, I should think. Would you like some coffee? I noticed that there was a drink's machine out there.'

Crista was about to refuse, then changed her mind. To be doing something, anything, would be better than doing nothing.

'Yes, thank you.'

'Right, I won't be a minute,' Hugo

said, giving her a quick smile.

Crista scarcely had time to wonder at the fact that she was sitting here waiting to see whether her father was going to be all right, with the man who undoubtedly must be his worst enemy, when Hugo was striding back into the room carrying two steaming cups of coffee.

'You'll feel better when you drink that,' he remarked handing her the cup. 'How is your ankle feeling, by the way?'

Crista gave him a tremulous smile, his sudden sympathy making her feel as if she could cry.

'Not too bad, thank you. I really haven't had time to dwell on it.'

'You should be resting it.'

He put his coffee down on the floor. 'This should help.'

He moved a couple of magazines off a stool and put it in front of her.

'You can rest your leg on that.'

Before Crista had a chance to protest, he'd lifted her injured leg and deposited it gently down on the stool. It did feel better.

'Thank you,' she said aloud, some-what grudgingly.

'My pleasure,' he replied.

The room fell quiet, and Crista actually jumped when there was a light tap at the door, and it opened to reveal a nurse. She spoke in Spanish.

'She wants you to go with her to see the doctor who has been attending to your father,' Hugo said when the nurse had stopped.

He then asked the nurse something in rapid Spanish.

'How is he? What's she saying?' Crista asked, feeling as if a tight hand was clutching at her heart. 'Is my father going to be all right?'

'Give her a chance to answer, Cristobel!' Hugo said.

The nurse spoke quickly, and Hugo translated straightaway.

'You've nothing to worry about. Your father is out of danger.'

'Thank goodness!' she exclaimed. 'I've been so worried.'

Hugo helped her to her feet,

encouraging her to lean heavily against him.

'I know you have, little one, but now everything's going to be just fine, just you wait and see.'

Then he turned to the nurse, and spoke in Spanish.

'Could you bring a wheelchair, please? As you can see, the young lady has an ankle injury. It's still difficult for her to walk any distance.'

A moment or two later, the nurse had returned with a chair, and Hugo was pushing her along a corridor.

'The nurse says that Dr Montego speaks good English, so I'll just bring you in to see him, and then I'll wait for you in the waiting-room.'

'I'm sure the hospital will call a taxi for me when I'm ready to leave.'

'My car is at your apartment anyway, Crista,' he reminded her. 'So I'll need to go back there to collect it. Apart from that, I don't want you wandering around on your own after the shock you've had and with an injured ankle.

Right, this is his room.'

He knocked at the door, and a moment or two later a small, wiry-looking man with greying black hair opened it. The two men exchanged a few words in Spanish, and then Dr Montego pushed Crista's wheelchair into the room.

'How is my father?' Crista asked immediately.

'He is going to be all right, but he is going to have to take more care of himself, to slow down. Your father, he has been doing too much. In fact, it surprises me greatly that something like this has not happened before.'

'Then it wasn't the fall which caused it?'

'Not at all. Your father, I think, is a man who has been suffering from considerable stress and strain. This puts great pressure on the heart.'

'But he is going to be all right, isn't he? What I mean is, he's not going to have another attack or anything like that?'

The doctor sat back in his chair and studied his fingertips.

'When a man has had a heart attack, it is always possible that he can have another,' he replied. 'It is a warning, if you like, a voice telling him that he must slow down, that he is no longer as young as he was.'

'How long will he have to stay in hospital?'

'Not long, probably just a few days. But he will not be fit to return to work straightaway. In fact, it is my opinion that your father could do with rest, and I suggest that he should go into a convalescent home for a time.'

'That's no problem, no problem at all,' Crista hurriedly assured him.

If only she'd taken more interest in the business before, had come out to Gran Canaria sooner, but no, she'd selfishly put her own career first, had only come when her father had pressurised her to do so.

'Is he conscious now? Can I see him?'

The doctor shook his head.

'He is sleeping quite normally now, and I do not wish that he is disturbed. You may, however, call in to see him tomorrow.'

Then he stood up, and Crista concluded that the interview was over. A nurse took her back to the room where Hugo was waiting, and he then went to call a taxi for them.

'What did Montego have to say?' Hugo wanted to know.

Crista started to tell him, and then broke off, hesitating. Should she tell him too much? After all, he was on the opposing side, their enemy. If he thought that her father was going to be out of the way for a while, wouldn't he try to take advantage of the fact?

'What's the matter, Crista, is there more?' Hugo prompted.

'No, nothing more,' Crista replied, quickly. 'Everything is going to be fine, just fine.'

Hugo looked as if he didn't believe her, but he let the matter go, for which

Crista was grateful.

Hugo paid the taxi driver when they reached her apartment, and swung Crista up in his arms.

'What are you doing?' she protested. 'I can walk you know, if you just let me lean on your arm.'

He shot her a disbelieving look.

'Up all those flights of stairs? I doubt it very much.'

Crista scowled. She'd forgotten that the lift was still out of order.

'Well, you can put me down as soon as we get up the stairs.'

In the event, he didn't.

'Aren't you going to invite me in?' he enquired, pausing with her in the doorway.

Crista threw him an exasperated look.

'No,' she said bluntly. 'Quite honestly, I feel as if I've had just about enough for one day.'

He set her down.

'I agree with you there, you certainly have. Well, if you're sure there's nothing more you want me to do.'

'Nothing at all, thank you. Actually, I just want to be alone.'

'OK then, I'll go. But make sure you rest.'

'I have every intention of doing just that,' she replied sweetly.

As he disappeared back down the stairs, she leaned against the closed door, only hobbling into the room when she heard his footsteps retreating. Then she sank down on to the settee.

What a day! She felt as if she'd aged ten years in the space of a few hours! What's more, she'd been forced to accept help from Hugo Santiago. And that was something she didn't want to do. He wasn't to be trusted.

She'd ring Roger and get him to come out to Gran Canaria and help her run Eastwood Travel. The more she thought about it, the better the idea sounded. Roger would be sure to get the hang of things very quickly, and, as he was still unemployed, he'd be glad of the opportunity to be in the sun and earn good money.

Fortunately, the phone was a portable one, so Crista was able to sit down while she put the call through to England. A female voice answered the phone. That was strange. Roger lived alone.

'Hello, may I speak to Roger Fortescue, please?' she asked.

'Who's calling?' the woman asked sharply.

'Crista.'

'Just a moment. Roger, there's someone called Crista on the line.'

And then Roger was there.

'Hello, sweetheart, how are you?'

Crista gave a mirthless laugh.

'I could be a lot better! Who was that who answered the phone?'

'Oh, you mean Sonia? Oh, she's just a friend of a friend. I don't think you've actually met her. Anyway, pet, what's new? Having a rip-roaring time out there, are you?'

Crista suppressed a shudder of distaste. Hadn't Roger heard what she'd said?

'Anything but, actually,' she replied, and quickly told him what had happened.

'Oh, hard luck, there! Anything I can do?'

'Well, actually there is.'

And she began to tell him of her idea.

'So, what do you think?'

'Not bad, not bad at all! Give me a day to think it over, will you? I'll get back to you first thing tomorrow. Now, I really must dash! 'Bye!'

Crista found she was still holding the receiver, listening to the impersonal sound of the dialling tone.

5

Had she done the right thing, Crista wondered, as she replaced the phone. Would she have been wiser just to rely on Stephen Jacobs, her father's assistant? But no, her father had always told her that family had to take an active part in the firm. Crista knew, also, that Stephen was attracted to her, and she certainly didn't want any further complications of the emotional kind. No, it would be better when Roger came out.

Surely he'd come, Crista thought as she made herself some coffee and toast, then after watching a movie she went off to bed. The day's events churned around her mind. It was so frustrating having an injured ankle, otherwise she'd have gone out and bought a newspaper. Certainly she needed to see one soon. Those awful headlines came back into her mind, Argentina Dangerous.

What would happen if her father was to inadvertently get hold of a copy? The shock would be enough to give him a second heart attack! But perhaps he already knew. Perhaps he'd already read the newspapers, so had already been in a more excitable state when he'd seen her with Hugo. That could well be it, and would partly explain why he'd had the heart attack.

Hugo Santiago had sold the story to the paper. What a hateful, unscrupulous thing to do. She sympathised with him about the loss of his little boy, but it didn't give him the right to tread randomly over other people.

Crista seethed with helpless anger against the man. Well, really, there was no reason why she should ever have to set eyes on him again. Crista knew that she should feel happy at the thought of not seeing Hugo again, yet, perversely, she didn't. Rather she felt as if something had passed out of her life and left it sadly lacking. Eventually, she fell into a troubled sleep, dreams of collapsing buildings and overflowing swimming pools even managing to invade her conscious mind.

Although she felt very tired the next morning, she was quite relieved to get up. Fortunately, her ankle was starting to feel a bit easier, and she managed her shower without too much trouble. She was just finishing a cup of coffee when the phone rang. That would be Roger, no doubt. But it wasn't, it was Stephen Jacobs.

'Crista, it's Stephen here. I'm sorry to trouble you so early. Your dad rang me up last night to tell me all about your injury, and then I got a copy of the paper. Young Gomez ought to be shot, photographing your fall like that, and yet doing nothing to rescue you! And the story! Have you seen the paper?'

'Only the headlines on a placard, but what was that you said about someone — Gomez, did you say his name was?'

'Yes. I wish I'd known about your accident sooner, I'd have come over yesterday to help you. I've been in touch with Gloria, and she said she'll call in to see if you want any shopping this morning.'

'Thanks, Stephen. I'm managing OK. My ankle feels a bit easier today.'

Perhaps she'd misjudged him, as he did seem to be quite thoughtful. But she had to know more about this mysterious Gomez.

'Who is Gomez, Stephen? Why was he taking photos?'

'Your father hired him to take some publicity shots of the Argentina, and it just happened that he caught your fall into the pool on film. After that, the rotten louse saw his chance and seized it. I don't doubt he's made quite a packet out of selling those pictures and his story to the papers.'

Then it hadn't been Hugo after all! She'd misjudged him. Crista's heart fluttered. She could see him again. Then she sobered just as quickly. All right, so he hadn't been so sneaky and downright underhanded as to sell information to the papers, but he was by no means innocent either. What innocent person would be in the Argentina grounds training binoculars on the place in the first place? She couldn't afford to forgive him so easily.

'What do you think will happen now, about the Argentina, I mean? Just how damaging is the article in the paper?' she went on to ask Stephen.

'Very, I'm afraid. Gomez as good as says that the whole place should be pulled down. He's insinuating that your father doesn't give a cuss about safety, that all he's interested in is showing a quick profit.

'Phew! What a terrible thing to happen, and it couldn't come at a worse time, either. You say Dad knows about all this?'

'Yes, it was your father who alerted me to it. I wouldn't be at all surprised if that's what brought on his heart attack.'

'Neither would I. Will the police be involved?'

'I don't know about the police, but

there's an inspector from the building department coming to see me this morning. I'll have to take him round the Argentina, and then I would imagine that they'd have surveyors and the like in. There's no way in which the place is going to be able to open in time. In fact, I've taken the liberty of placing an announcement in next week's paper, and the tourist magazine, saying the reception party has been cancelled.'

'Good, Stephen, that was the right thing to do. Of course, people will talk, but I can't see how we can avoid that. What time is the inspector coming round this morning?'

'Ten o'clock.'

Crista glanced at her watch. It was gone nine-thirty now.

'Look, Stephen, I'll have to dash. I want to be there when that fellow comes. The appointment is at the Margarita, I take it.'

'Yes, but Crista, there's no need. I can take care of it. Stay there and rest your ankle. As I said, Gloria will be calling.'

'No, Stephen,' Crista interrupted. 'With my father away, I'm in charge, and I intend to be there when the fate of the Argentina is settled. 'Bye for now, I'll see you in about a quarter of an hour.'

And before Stephen could protest further, she'd replaced the receiver, and called a taxi to pick her up in ten minutes. Then it was a frantic dash into the bedroom, where she slipped into a smart, navy and white spotted dress and matching white sandals. She just applied the merest touch of foundation and lipstick. She was combing her hair, when the telephone rang. Should she answer it? She didn't really have time, but this time it was sure to be Roger, so perhaps she'd better.

'Hello, and how is my favourite girl?' Roger's familiar tones asked.

Strange how even his voice was starting to irritate her. It sounded false and somehow ingratiating.

'Hello, Roger. Look, I'm in a dreadful hurry. Can I call you back later?'

'Don't you even want to know what I've decided?'

Roger sounded rather huffy.

'Of course I do!' she cried, hurriedly, and at the same time, the taxi hooted outside. 'Oh, gosh, that's my taxi now. I've got to go up to the Margarita. There's an inspector coming there and then he wants to look round the Argentina. Well, what have you decided, Roger? Quickly.'

'If you're really sure you really want me to, then I'll come. But I must say, you don't sound as if you're that bothered.'

'Of course I am, Roger. That's wonderful news. It's just that I don't have the time to talk right now. I'll call you back to discuss all the details just as soon as I can. 'Bye for now.'

And so she left Roger hanging on the line just as he'd left her the previous evening. She arrived at the Margarita just on ten o'clock. Gloria was in the office, and greeted her warmly, although Crista thought she looked worried, not her normal, cool, poised self at all.

'The man from the government is in Stephen's office,' she said, keeping her voice low. 'You want to go in there now? You're sure that it wouldn't be better to leave it to Stephen? He knows all about the building.'

'I have to go in, Gloria. I have to try and take Father's place.'

'I understand, but it is a pity that you do not have a strong man behind you. I warned you against El Diablo, and yet, at this time, I cannot help but wish that he and your father were on better terms. He is a very strong character, that hombre, and he would know how to treat government man!'

Despite the levity of the situation, Crista couldn't help smiling.

'This is a turn-about, Gloria. I thought that you thought that Hugo was a trouble-maker who should be

110

avoided at all costs.'

'He's had too much tragedy in his life, and that does strange things to a man, makes him embittered, hardens him. I was also worried because you are so much like Marianne, and I didn't know how he would cope with the memories which your physical resemblance must bring. But he is a strong man, who fears nothing. That is the type you need in a situation like this.'

This was the time when Crista could have told Gloria that Roger would be coming out to run the business, but, curiously, she didn't. Somehow, when she compared Roger with Hugo, Roger came out somewhat lacking.

'Oh, well, he's not here, and never likely to be, so this is something which I'll just have to face myself, Gloria. Keep your fingers crossed for me!'

'I will be glad to. Good luck.'

'Thanks, Gloria.'

Crista limped over to the door. She rapped on it firmly, and then, without waiting to be told to come in, she entered. Stephen was sitting behind his large, mahogany desk, and a heavy, thickset man was facing him. Crista couldn't see the stranger's face, but if Stephen's expression was anything to go by, the interview wasn't going too well.

'Ah, this is Miss Cristobel Eastwood, John Eastwood's daughter.'

Stephen was on his feet, pulling out a chair for Crista, as the government inspector turned and looked at her. He had a cold, hard face, with thick, horn-rimmed glasses. Crista gave an involuntary shudder.

'This is a nasty business that you find yourself in, Miss Eastwood.'

His voice was harsh, with only a faint trace of an accent, and one which she couldn't place. He certainly didn't sound, or look, Spanish.

'This is Mr Lars Eriksson,' Stephen announced, and Crista assumed that the unpleasant inspector originated from one of the Scandinavian countries.

'It's a very unpleasant business, yes.

But I think that you'll find the Press has blown things out of all proportion,' she said as calmly as she could.

'You think so? Well, we shall see. Now, I really don't think that there is much that we can discuss here. Better that we go to the infamous Argentina so that I can see for myself what secrets it holds.'

'As you wish,' Crista replied, coolly. 'Stephen, do you want to take my father's car, or would you prefer to ring for a taxi?'

'We'll go in my car.'

He turned to the inspector and added, 'That is if you have no objection.'

'I'll take my own car and follow you there. That way I can get back to my office and file my report all the quicker.'

'Just as you wish,' Crista said matter-of-factly.

'We're not going to get much joy from this one,' Stephen remarked, grimly, as they drove to the Argentina.

'He's already condemned us without

a trial, hasn't he?' Crista replied.

'I'm afraid he has. Still, if he's too unfair, we could probably ask for a second assessment. Mind you, whether we'd get it is another thing. Things aren't done quite like home out here.'

As he spoke, Stephen pulled into the Argentina carpark, and they got out of the car and waited for Lars Eriksson on the steps of the building. To her immense frustration, Crista found that her ankle just wasn't up to accompanying them on their tour of the building, and she was forced to wait in the foyer until they returned, some length of time later. She saw at once that Stephen was grim-faced, but that the inspector was actually smiling.

'Well?' she demanded, her heart leaping into her mouth.

'I have seen all I need to see,' Lars Eriksson replied. 'As of now, the Argentina is forbidden to open pending an official enquiry. Defy me at your peril!' he added before turning away and heading back to his car.

Stephen wanted to take Crista out for lunch, but she refused, she was just too upset. Instead, she requested that he drop her off back at the office in the Margarita, and go off for his own lunch break. She told Gloria briefly what had happened, and then sent her off for lunch, too. Then she went into her father's office, slumped in his chair, and closed her eyes. She was so engrossed in her melancholy thoughts, that she didn't hear the knock at the door, didn't look up, in fact, until she was aware someone was in the room. She started visibly.

Hugo Santiago was standing there, looking down at her with a look of such infinite kindness on his handsome face that she almost disgraced herself by bursting into tears. But not quite. After all, she was an Eastwood, her father's daughter. She had to keep hold of some pride.

'You look absolutely shattered,' he remarked, without preamble.

Then, without waiting for her to give

him permission, he was sitting down across the desk from her.

'What are you doing here, anyway? You should still be at home resting. Your ankle's not going to get better this way.'

'My ankle's the very least of my problems,' Crista replied wearily.

'Want to tell me about it?'

Crista shook her head. What was there to tell? He was in competition with her father, so he'd hear soon enough, and the situation must surely only be to his advantage. However pleasant he seemed to be trying to be to her at the moment, she just wasn't in the mood for it; she'd had enough.

'Why don't you just go away and leave me alone?' she asked.

'Well, for one reason, I don't want to, and, if you need another, you don't look in any fit condition to be left here alone. Have you eaten?'

'No, and I don't want to.'

'Nevertheless, you should.'

He got up, and pulled her to her feet.

'Come on, there's a pleasant little restaurant just round the corner from here. If I recollect correctly, they do some excellent pizzas, and you're rather fond of those, aren't you?'

'Today, I'm not fond of anything,' Crista snapped back at him, although she knew she was being unjust.

Nevertheless, she allowed him to lead her from the office.

'I'm very sorry about your father,' Hugo remarked gently, after they'd ordered two pizzas and mineral water. 'He's the kind of man who will chafe at not being able to do anything.'

Crista bristled.

'And are you sorry about his hotel, too? Are you sorry that the Argentina's not allowed to open pending enquiry?'

In her distress, she'd forgotten her previous resolution not to tell him.

'Is that what's happened? Well, I can't really admit to being too surprised, but I didn't think that it would be so soon.'

'The government inspector's been there this morning. He was most 'definite, I'm afraid.'

'Does your father know?' he enquired, face serious.

'No,' Crista replied. 'I've only just found out myself.'

How on earth was she going to break this news to him? Another shock could prove fatal. Hugo seemed to read her thoughts.

'I would have said not to tell him, but being your father, he's bound to find out,' he said, with a wry smile. 'After we've finished lunch, I'll take you to hospital to see him. It might help to have moral support.'

'Thanks, Hugo, but, no. I can't honestly think that seeing you is going to make him feel any better.'

'No, I suppose you're right. But I could still take you there and wait for you, if you'll permit me to.'

His voice was curiously humble, and Crista looked at him in surprise.

'Why do you want to?' she asked. 'I thought you'd have been gloating, seeing Eastwood Travel is your main business competitor. With us in the doldrums, things can only get better for your firm.'

Hugo sighed.

'I'm not your enemy, Crista, even though you seem to think so. All right, I have to admit that I had grave misgivings about the Argentina. It was built far too quickly, with no thought for safety. Your father was only interested in keeping costs down, and being competitive in the bulk tourist market.'

Crista's eyes had darkened with anger, but she couldn't reply right away, as the waiter was putting their meals in front of them. OK, so Hugo probably did have a point, obviously, in view of what had happened. But how could she bring herself to agree with him? It was too disloyal to her father.

'As I told the man from the government, I think all this business has been blown up out of all proportion. If the place hadn't been safe, then the tour companies wouldn't have been so anxious to feature it in their brochures.

It's booked up solidly for the next three months.'

She broke off.

Oh, no! Where were all those tourists going to go now? The Margarita was a much more up-market place, and she would have to try and fit as many as possible there, and charge them the much lower rate. Such a move would certainly bite deeply into the resources of the company. And, even worse, there was no way that she could possibly accommodate them all. The Margarita was a far smaller hotel than the Argentina.

6

We're going to have to work something out, Crista,' Hugo said gently. 'You'll need to talk to your accountants. Find out just what Eastwood Travel's assets are. I may need to know, if I'm going to help you.'

'I don't need your help. I'm quite capable of managing. Stephen has been in the business for the last couple of years, and Roger's coming out here to help me.'

Hugo leaned back in his chair, a cynical smile curving his lips.

'Are you going straight to the hospital when we leave here? If so, my offer to bring you there still stands.'

'No, I'm going back to the office first, to ring Roger.'

Hugo's lips tightened ever so slightly.

'Very well, then, if I can't be of any further service to you, I'll just walk you back there and ring you this evening to find out how your father is.'

Back at the office, Crista discovered Roger had booked on a plane leaving Heathrow at ten o'clock the following morning.

'I'll be in at around two o'clock. You'll meet me at the airport, will you?'

'If I can drive. I haven't tried since I sprained my ankle.'

She went on to tell him about the balcony giving way, and falling into the icy waters of the Argentina pool. Roger whistled through his teeth.

'My poor Crista! You have been having a bad time of it! It's a good job that fellow saw you. What did you say his name was?'

'Hugo Santiago. Yes, I know it was, but I can't help but wonder what he was doing there, with binoculars trained on the place.'

'Sizing it up, I guess. You did say he was the opposition, didn't you?'

Crista heard a female voice in the background.

'Is there someone with you?' she asked.

Roger gave a slightly nervous giggle. 'Why ever should you think that?'

'Because I can hear a voice in the background,' she said pointedly.

At the same time, she was surprised to find that she felt no sense at all of jealousy, only a mild curiosity.

'Oh, it's just the lady from the laundry. I had some shirts and suits laundered. So here they are, express delivery!'

Somehow, she didn't quite believe him. Never mind, she had more than enough on her plate at the moment to feel too concerned as to what Roger was up to. He was coming out to help her, that was the main thing.

'If I can, I'll meet you tomorrow, if not, I'll get Stephen to come. Stephen's my father's manager,' she added briefly.

'Well, I hope you don't expect me to work under him. I got the impression when you called that you wanted me to take over the managerial rôle.'

'You can hardly walk straight in there and run the whole show without the slightest bit of experience. I know you're very intelligent, Roger, but even you need to get some idea of what's what before you can take over. Anyway, I must go now. I have to go to the hospital to see how Dad is. I'll see you tomorrow. And thank you for coming. I'm glad you've decided to.'

But was she, Crista asked herself, as they said their goodbyes, and she replaced the receiver. Well, now was not the time to dwell on it. There was too much to do. She stopped by at Stephen's office to tell him that she was going to the hospital, but that she'd be back in a couple of hours, and then he could give her some information about how Eastwood Travel was actually doing. Stephen passed a hand through his hair.

'Let me take you out to dinner this evening. By the time you get back here, it's not going to be worth starting on the books. I think it would be better if you come in early tomorrow morning, and we go over them together then. But, in the meantime, I can fill you in with a few things tonight.'

Crista hesitated. She had no great desire to have dinner with him, and yet she had to admit that there was sense in what he said. She nodded, managing a slight smile.

'OK, Stephen, that sounds like a good idea.'

'Right then, I'll call for you just before eight. Are you going to take a taxi to the hospital. It might be a bit difficult for you driving.'

'No, I want to try and see what it's like.'

She briefly explained about Roger coming out the following day, and that she'd promised to pick him up at the airport, ankle permitting. Stephen frowned.

'I suppose I can understand you wanting your boyfriend here at a time like this, Crista, but do you really think it's wise to involve him in the business? I don't mean to be presumptuous, but does he actually know anything about this kind of work?'

Crista should have been annoyed, but strangely enough, she wasn't. Probably because she was wondering the same thing herself.

'He's very clever,' she said. 'I'm sure he'll soon learn.'

'Well, if you think so, all right then, Crista. I'll call for you later. Give my best wishes to your father, and if you have any trouble driving, come back in here and ring for a taxi.'

Crista actually found driving easier than she'd expected, and was at the hospital within ten minutes. She stopped at the door of his room and knocked. A surprisingly strong voice called.

'Come in!'

Crista found her father propped up with several pillows. He was rather pale, but apart from that, looked better than she'd dared to hope.

'So, it's you, girl!' he barked at her. 'Taken you long enough to get here, hasn't it?'

Crista pulled up a chair and sat down.

'How are you feeling, Dad?'

'Less of the sentimental nonsense, Cristobel,' he exclaimed, looking quite irritated. 'You know it doesn't wash with me. Well, it's a fine mess we've got ourselves into this time, eh? The Argentina not safe indeed! That place is every bit as safe as the Gran Palacio.'

The Gran Palacio was probably the finest hotel in Gran Canaria, and it belonged to Hugo Santiago! Crista managed a tremulous smile.

'Well, perhaps not quite, Dad! After all, the Argentina does seem to have quite a few things needing attention before it'll be fit to open.'

'What are you trying to tell me, girl? Are you telling me that you believe all that filthy rubbish they've printed in the papers? Lies, all of it! It's the work of that wretched Gomez. I should never have trusted the scoundrel to take pictures of the Argentina in the first place.'

'Don't get yourself so excited, Dad,' Crista said worriedly. 'You have to slow down and take things a lot easier.'

'I'll tell you one thing, my girl. I'm not staying here a day longer than I absolutely have to! The Argentina's official opening is less than a fortnight away, and I admit that there are a few things to be put right before then. Stephen tries, but this calls for someone strong at the helm.'

Clearly, her father thought that the Argentina was still going to open as scheduled. How on earth was she going to tell him that that very morning Lars Eriksson had slapped a closing order on it? To tell him this could easily provoke a further attack. But if she didn't tell him, he'd be sure to find out, possibly reading it for himself in the papers.

Perhaps she should talk to Dr Montego first, ask him how she should go about breaking this further unwelcome news to her father.

'Is Dr Montego on duty today, Dad?' she asked suddenly.

John Eastwood shot her a look of surprise.

'Why do you want to know?' he asked suspiciously. 'Is there something going on that I don't know about?'

Crista forced a smile.

'No, of course not. I want to have a little chat with him, check on your progress and such like.'

'Well, maybe it's not such a bad idea. You could tell him that you think I'm ready to leave here first thing in the morning. I'll ring for the nurse and she can take you to see Montego. Have you been to the office this morning?' he asked, as they waited for the nurse to come.

'Yes,' Crista replied guardedly, not wishing to reveal what had actually gone on there, how Lars Eriksson had inspected the Argentina, and put his closing order on it.

'Everything all right there, was it?' he asked.

'Well, I haven't really had time to learn very much yet. Stephen is taking me out for dinner tonight, a business dinner,' she added hastily. 'I'm not in the least interested in Stephen.'

A moment or two later, a nurse appeared.

'How are you feeling now, Senor Eastwood? You wanted something?'

'I'll be a lot better when I get out of this place,' John Eastwood grumbled. 'But, no, I don't want anything at the moment, just for you to take my daughter to Dr Montego. She wants a few words with him.'

'Well, I will have to see if the doctor is available and can see her first. When I've found out, I'll ring through and let you know.'

Dr Montego agreed to see Crista straightaway, probably because her father was a private patient and paying a good deal of money for his treatment, she reflected, a trifle cynically, as she was once again shown into his room. The doctor rose, bowed to Crista, and indicated that she should take a seat opposite him.

'Senorita Eastwood, I am happy to see you again,' he began. 'Your father is making very satisfactory progress. I'll want him to remain here tomorrow, but I think that the following day he should be fit enough to go to a convalescent home. I have particulars of one here which I think you will find to be suitable.'

He handed her a brochure. Crista put it into her handbag without looking at it, then, rightly interpreting the doctor's questioning expression, she explained.

'I'll look at it later and let you know when I come in to see my father tomorrow morning. But that's not why I wanted to see you. You see, I've got some very difficult news to break to my father, and I was wondering if you could give me any advice as to how I should do it.'

She explained about the government closure of the Argentina, and how much the hotel meant to her father.

'Your father is not, I think, the kind

of man who would welcome news being held back from him, so my advice to you is to tell him as quickly, and as briefly as possible. If you wish, I will do this for you, yet I think, as his daughter, it would be better coming from you.'

'I agree,' Crista said, standing up. 'There's no chance that it could precipitate another heart attack, is there, Doctor?'

Dr Montego shook his head.

'No, my dear, that would be highly unlikely given the medication that he is on. His blood pressure was very high, but we have that stabilised, and he is also having mild sedatives for the time being.'

'Thank you, Doctor Montego, you've helped to set my mind at rest.'

And without giving herself further time to think about it, Crista went back to her father's room to break the news to him.

7

It hadn't been as bad as she'd expected, Crista reflected, as she put the finishing touches to her make-up in anticipation of Stephen's arrival that evening. In fact, it was almost as if her father had expected it.

He had complained, and cursed the entire Spanish government, but he had understood that even he couldn't do anything about it. He had, however, been adamant about wanting to see Stephen as soon as possible. Crista had wanted to know why, but he had been unusually unforthcoming and insisted he see Stephen alone.

So, as there seemed little more to say, she'd made her goodbyes, told him to take care, and said that she'd be in to see him the following morning. She hadn't told him about Roger's imminent arrival in Gran Canaria, having reasoned that one shock was quite enough for one day!

At that moment, the doorbell trilled. That would be Stephen now. As she walked towards the door, Crista couldn't help but gaze at the phone, which had remained disappointingly quiet all evening despite Hugo's promise to ring and ask her how her father was.

Ah, well, she supposed that was a further indication of the fact that he just couldn't be trusted. Crista was so sure that it would be Stephen, that she didn't bother to use the security chain, just pulled the heavy door open. Then she stepped back in shock, for standing there in the doorway, looking larger than life, was Hugo Santiago.

'What are you doing here?' she stammered.

Hugo smiled.

'May I come in?'

'Well, actually, it's not very convenient at the moment,' she began.

'Nonsense!' he interrupted her, stepping past her and into the apartment.

Crista had no option but to close the door and turn towards him.

'You really are the limit,' she exclaimed. 'I told you it wasn't convenient, yet you just interrupt me and barge straight in! Well, you'll have to go again, Hugo, because Stephen will be here any minute. He's taking me out to dinner, a business dinner,' she added.

'Oh, no, he's not,' Hugo stated positively. 'I am!'

'What on earth are you talking about? Have you taken leave of your senses? I just told you, I've already arranged to see Stephen.'

'And Stephen won't be coming. He's otherwise engaged.'

'Do you think you could stop talking in riddles for a few minutes and tell me just what's going on?'

Crista's indignation was rising by the minute.

'Stephen is presently holding an emergency convention with your father, and the Eastwood Travel accountant, at the hospital, at your father's instigation. I called the hospital to find out how your father was, and they put me through to his room. Stephen answered the phone. He was quite upset about letting you down tonight and, believe it or not, your father suggested that I should take his place.'

He spread his hands expressively.

'So there you have it. You've been ordered to go out with me whether you like it or not.'

Crista shook her head.

'No, I don't believe it. It's just some ridiculous scheme that you and Stephen have concocted between you to somehow put me at a disadvantage. Well, I'm not going!' she spluttered.

'Oh, yes, you are.' Hugo's voice was silky. 'I've made a booking at the Sombrero. It's in Mogan, remember, and you liked it there. Now, be a good girl and come along. We don't want to keep the restaurant waiting.'

'I'm going nowhere with you, Mr Santiago. And how dare you say that it was my father's suggestion. He'd die before he'd ask you to take me out!'

'I am not a liar,' he replied. 'It was your father's suggestion, but if you want to let the restaurant down, and go hungry, then suit yourself!'

He turned sharply on his heel and headed for the door. Crista hesitated. Just suppose he had been telling the truth? Just suppose that for some reason best known to himself, her father did actually want her to have dinner with Hugo? And what of herself? If she was to be truthful, didn't she want to go? Didn't the prospect fill her with far more joy and anticipation than a business dinner with Stephen?

'Wait!' she cried. 'If you still want me to, I'll come.'

The next second, before she had any idea of what he was about to do, he'd swept her up into his arms, so that her feet were lifted off the ground. His lips brushed hers fleetingly.

'Of course I want you to come. Very, very much!'

As they set out along the coast road, she turned to Hugo.

'But why did my father want you to take me out?'

'Perhaps he likes me,' Hugo replied with an enigmatic smile.

'Oh, I doubt that,' Crista exclaimed.

Hugo chuckled.

'Why? I assure you, I can be a very likeable person.'

'Well, I hardly think that my father likes you! Oh, I don't mean you personally, rather what you stand for.'

'Ah, I see! The old family quarrel rearing its ugly head again?'

This time Crista's shiver was so noticeable that Hugo remarked on it.

'Are you cold, little one?' he asked. 'I can always turn up the heater.'

'Oh, no, it's not that,' she exclaimed.

Now he'd know that the shiver which had shaken her entire body was because of him! He laughed softly.

'You're not as unaware of me as you like to pretend, are you?'

'You certainly know how to make

your presence felt.'

'I meant as a man, Cristobel. You're not unaware of me as a man, are you? Despite your Roger.'

'I don't think this conversation is achieving anything,' Crista exclaimed, feeling thoroughly hot and bothered.

Fortunately, by this time, they'd reached the carpark.

'The restaurant is just across the road, by the harbour,' Hugo remarked, getting out of the car and coming over to Crista's side to open the door.

She took his arm, and they walked the short distance, Crista limping only slightly, and she thought how different it was from a couple of days ago when they'd visited Mogan and her ankle had been so painful that he'd had to half carry her.

'You're very silent,' Hugo remarked, after they'd entered the restaurant. 'You're not still cross at your change of escort, are you? I really wouldn't have thought that Stephen, likeable enough as he is, was your type.'

'He's not. But as I told you, it was only to be a business dinner.'

'And what was the business going to be about, I wonder,' he enquired, as they sat down at a corner table.

Crista was irritated.

'Oh, and wouldn't you like to know! Anything to make matters still worse for Eastwood Travel, and glorify Voyager still further!'

Hugo sighed.

'My dear Crista, I was only trying to help. But never mind, let this be a night for relaxation. Let's forget business and concentrate on being friends. What are you going to have to eat?'

He was calling a truce, and she knew that she must, at least temporarily, do likewise. To do anything else would seem very churlish.

'I thought I'd have the prawn cocktail to start, and then the grilled sole.'

'Yes, that's a good choice. I'll have the same. And to drink? You have, perhaps, some wine you prefer?'

Crista shook her head.

'I prefer white to red, but I'll leave the choice to you.'

A moment or two later a waiter came and took their order.

'So, Crista, your boyfriend arrives tomorrow. Are you looking forward to seeing him?'

'Well, of course I am!'

Crista stiffened, partly because it wasn't really true, in fact, she'd temporarily forgotten the fact that Roger was coming at all, and it gave her a faintly nasty jolt to be reminded of it, particularly by Hugo.

'Will he stay long?' Hugo continued.

'As long as is necessary,' Crista replied.

'Necessary for what?' he wanted to know.

'To look after the business until my father gets back, I suppose.'

Hugo leaned back in his seat. He looked totally relaxed, smiling.

'This is interesting news. So the brilliant Roger is going to take over the running of Eastwood Travel! Voyager will have to watch out.'

'Why don't we stop talking business and get on with our meal,' she burst out. 'Anyway, I thought you were going to tell me more about your ex-wife, about Marianne,' she continued, recklessly. 'We never did seem to get to discuss her when you took me out to lunch in Mogan before.'

It was her way of getting her own back. He'd pursued the subject of Roger when she hadn't wanted to talk about him, and she was still curious about the woman whom she resembled. He grimaced. Quite obviously the subject was distasteful to him, and Crista felt a momentary twinge of guilt.

'If I do that, I'm likely to choke on my prawn cocktail,' he replied, and began eating.

In fact, he didn't say anything else until they'd both finished.

'Right then, Crista, so what is it you want to know? Didn't Gloria fill you in sufficiently?'

The way he phrased it made her feel as if she was being extraordinarily nosy, prying into things which were none of her concern, and which could only cause him pain.

'I'm sorry. Obviously it's still difficult for you to talk about her, so perhaps it's better if I don't say any more.'

Did he still care for Marianne, despite what had happened? Was that why he seemed to want to see Crista, although by doing so, he was only hurting himself . . . and her. Hugo seemed to have read her mind, as he replied.

'I was in love with my ex-wife once, but believe me, the feelings I had for her didn't last. Our marriage was over long before she left me. In fact, I didn't care that she'd gone. I was glad. The only thing that bothered me was that she took Robin with her. And even if it wasn't by her own hand, she killed him, and I'll never forgive her for that. But it's in the past, and should remain buried.'

You should talk about it, Crista wanted to protest, stop bottling it up,

like an overflowing dam that can find
no release. But she didn't dare. He
looked too formidable. Fortunately, at
that moment, the waiter came and took
their plates away, and the stormy
tension which had hung over them
gradually receded. Hugo chose that
moment to change the subject.

'I know I promised not to talk
business, but I do have a suggestion to
put to you.'

'Oh? What is it?'

'That some of the tourists you have
booked for the Argentina can stay at my
hotels.'

'Thank you for your offer,' she
replied. 'I'll discuss it with Stephen, and
Roger when he gets here, then I'll get
back to you and let you know.'

She'd put it almost as if she was
bestowing a favour on him, yet she was
very well aware that it was actually he
who would be doing Eastwood Travel a
great favour, and she couldn't help but
wonder why he should want to. After
all, what was in it for him? Voyager

Travel was most definitely up-market, and didn't boast anything less than four-star hotels in the Canaries.

The money that the tour companies were paying Eastwood Travel for their holidaymakers to stay at the Argentina would be far less than what Hugo's hotels would demand. But perhaps that was it. Perhaps his hotels weren't really doing so well, and he was counting on Eastwood Travel supplying guests to fill empty rooms. Worse still, he might well expect her father's company to make up the difference financially.

'No, we're not short of guests,' he said, seeming to read her thoughts. 'But we do own quite a number of hotels throughout the Canaries, so there are always some vacancies as long as your visitors are prepared to be flexible as to which island they actually go to. I think you'll find they will be. After all, they'll be getting a much better standard of accommodation for a far cheaper price.'

'But what about you? You're not a charity. What's in it for you? Or do you expect us to make up the difference? Because, if so, we'd probably be better to look around for budget accommodation in Gran Canaria.'

'I'll be filling my empty rooms, and with that, I'll be satisfied. You don't seem to realise, Crista, but I do want to help you.'

'But why should you want to help me?' she persisted.

He didn't reply at once, partly because the waiter reappeared with their main courses, and also because he wasn't immediately sure what to say.

'You've had more than your fair share of bad luck, and you're plucky,' he said at last, when the waiter had retired. 'I'd also like to see our families on a better footing, and I think your father is starting to feel that way, too.'

'Because he suggested you take me out this evening, you mean?'

'People change, Crista,' he replied, enigmatically.

It was obvious that she wasn't going to get anything further out of him at the moment, so, following his lead, Crista began on her meal.

'That was gorgeous, but I'm so full!' she exclaimed at last, pushing a nearly empty plate away from her. 'I couldn't eat another thing.'

He grinned.

'OK, how about two Irish coffees?'

'Well, I suppose I can just about manage that.'

They lingered over their coffees for a good half hour. Hugo was an interesting, witty companion, and Crista found herself enjoying his company.

It was a jolt, therefore, when he said, 'I don't want to sound like a real saviour, but I've a suspicion that your father's finances aren't very sound.'

'Why? What makes you say that?' she asked, annoyed to find that there was a slight tremble in her voice.

'One hears rumours. But we could, perhaps, come to some agreement, but I'd want you to send your friend Roger back home.'

Crista was looking at him in horror.

'This dinner has been some sort of a set-up, hasn't it? How much my father and Stephen are involved, I don't know, but believe me, I intend to find out first thing in the morning. And, now, Mr Santiago, I would appreciate it if you'd take me home. You've just managed to spoil what could have been an enjoyable evening.'

'Just as you wish,' he agreed, irritatingly affable, as he asked for the bill. 'Don't you even want to know what my suggestion is?'

'No, thank you. I don't trust you an inch. Anything you'd tell me would be sure to be just a distortion of the truth! Anyway, as I said, if my father or Stephen have had any part in this, I'll find out from them.'

'I'll leave it for Stephen or your father to tell you tomorrow.'

'You know, I expect, that you are the most infuriating man that I've had the misfortune to lay eyes on!' Crista exclaimed furiously, as she followed him out of the restaurant.

He turned then, and took her arm, smiling down at her.

'No doubt you're right, but what else can you expect of a man known as El Diablo, the devil?'

8

Crista was up bright and early the next day, and despite the fact that it was only just after eight when she arrived at the hotel, Stephen was already in his office. He looked very tired, and judging from the mountain of books on his desk, and the active computer screen, he'd been working for quite some time. It was Stephen who spoke first.

'Hi. You're here early, Crista! I'm really sorry about last night, but as I expect Hugo told you, I was rather tied up.'

Crista sank down on to a chair.

'So I gather,' she said. 'All right, I forgive you for sending Hugo instead, but just what is going on?'

'We can't afford to antagonise Hugo, Crista. He could very well be the only lifeline we have. Eastwood Travel is heavily in debt, has been for some time,' he replied, without preamble. 'Your father was banking on the Argentina making things right, but without that . . . '

His voice trailed off, and he spread his hands helplessly.

'Hugo's prepared to take over the company.'

Stephen's words were like a death knell to Crista's ears.

'There is a proviso, of course. He doesn't want your friend Roger here.'

'He's got a terrible cheek!' she exclaimed. 'Apart from my own feelings on the matter, there's no way in which my father would ever agree to such a preposterous suggestion!'

'I think he would,' Stephen said glumly.

'Things are that bad?' she asked.

Stephen nodded. And for the next couple of hours they both pored over books until Crista felt that her eyes were popping and her brain was spinning. Stephen was right though. If Eastwood Travel was to have any hope at all of survival, they were going to need a huge cash injection.

'There must be some other way!' Crista's voice was frantic.

'The company is already mortgaged up to the hilt,' Stephen said. 'It's just a pity that your friend Roger is already on his way out here, because Hugo won't allow him to take any part in the running of the company.'

'But why? What's Roger ever done to him? He doesn't even know him!'

'I'd have thought that was obvious. Hugo Santiago is in love with you.'

Crista shook her head, not actually trusting herself to speak.

'Oh, but that's quite ridiculous!' she cried. 'Oh, no, Stephen, you're quite wrong there. If anything, Hugo Santiago hates me!'

'Maybe he does, sometimes. But hatred is akin to love.'

'I don't believe you! Anyway, I'm going to talk to my father.'

'Try not to upset your father too much. The meeting we had last night went on to almost ten o'clock, in fact, it would probably have continued longer if a nurse hadn't appeared and told Rodriguez, the accountant, and myself that your father desperately needed rest and that she wouldn't be answerable for the consequences unless we left.'

'I do wish he'd forget the wretched company for once in his life and concentrate on getting better.'

'More reason for you to let Hugo take over.'

'My father's got the final say, and he'll never agree, I know it.'

'Oh, no. Last night he signed an agreement which gives you total say, in his absence, for any decisions concerning Eastwood Travel.'

Crista was astonished.

'He knows he's not up to it at the moment, Crista, so he's done the only thing he could do. After all, you are his heir. But the agreement is only for a temporary period until he regains his health. I think he's just trying to show that he cares for you and trusts you.'

'I just don't know what to say any more. Anyway, don't do anything until I tell you. But I suppose you can't, can you? Not if I've got the final say!'

When Crista arrived at the hospital she was told her father was sedated.

'Why?' Crista demanded worriedly. 'He's not worse, is he?'

'I will put you through to Dr Montego and you can speak to him.'

Fortunately, Dr Montego was in his office, and she was able to speak to him straightaway.

'Don't worry, Miss Eastwood, it is only a safety measure. Your father exerted himself far too much last evening. Leave him to sleep today, and then you can come tomorrow morning, and, as long as he is well enough, he may leave for the Las Palomas convalescent home.'

Crista knew he was right, so she made no further protest. Things weren't going to be easy, but somehow, she'd just have to manage them herself.

Oh, why had she phoned Roger and asked him to come to Gran Canaria, she wondered, as she made her way back to her car. Habit, she supposed. She'd been dating Roger for the past eighteen months, and she'd acted purely on impulse. She hadn't missed him, and she was forced to face the fact that although she'd imagined herself to be in love with him, that was all it was, imagination.

Oh, she'd admired his intelligence, been flattered, even, that such a brilliant person could want her. But what was he doing with his life? He'd left university four years ago and still didn't have a job. And she began to see now that was largely because he hadn't wanted one. Roger was quite happy for her to pay for him on most occasions when they went out. Even his fare to Gran Canaria was being financed by Eastwood Travel. So, should she really be feeling so guilty? He could have a free holiday. She'd already arranged for him to stay at the Margarita, and then he could return to England, no harm done.

The plane from London arrived exactly on schedule, but Roger must have been delayed a bit in collecting his baggage, because it was over an hour after the flight's arrival was displayed on the Arrivals notice board that Roger actually stepped out from customs. Crista's heart sank to her feet as she took one look at the angry expression which marred his face. She rushed forward, and spoke, with an enthusiasm she was far from feeling.

'Hi. It's lovely to see you! How was your flight?'

'The flight was all right. It's what's happened afterwards.'

'What do you mean?'

'Oh, just fetch a trolley, will you, darling? I'll tell you all about it when we go out to the car.'

Crista obediently fetched a trolley. She could guess what had happened to Roger at customs. He'd been searched! She had to admit that her father had a point. Although it was a rather dated word, Roger did look like a hippy and a bit sinister and he did not tolerate authority. She wondered how she'd ever managed to stand him for eighteen months, never mind imagining that she was in love with him.

'That's a relief!' Roger sighed, as he hoisted the huge case on to the trolley, along with a sizeable flight bag.

'You have brought a lot of things,' Crista said.

'Not really,' Roger replied. 'After all, I've absolutely no idea how long I'm going to be staying for, so it's better to have too much than too little.'

Crista had a feeling that Roger's stay wasn't going to be nearly as long as he seemed to imagine, but she felt that now wasn't the right time to tell him. Perhaps after she had him back at the Margarita, after he'd had a shower and a meal and was feeling more relaxed, she'd speak to him.

'Those customs people were the absolute end!' Roger exclaimed, bitterly, as they made their way to the carpark. 'The wretched machine bleeped when I went through, just because I had a couple of keys in my pocket, but they didn't seem to believe me, and, would you believe it, searched me! I've never felt so humiliated in my life, and, at the end of it all, they didn't even have the manners to say sorry, just told me I could go.'

'They can be a bit strict sometimes,' Crista agreed, hoping that her voice sounded suitably sympathetic, although, in truth, she was finding it increasingly difficult to feel any sympathy at all for Roger, at last realising what a selfish, shallow person he actually was.

'Jolly nice car you have here, Crista,' he remarked, climbing into the neat little sports car which her father had provided her with. Temporarily, at least, Roger's equilibrium seemed to be restored, Crista observed, as she switched on the ignition and they pulled out of the airport carpark.

'Boy, but it's hot out here! Still, I think it's going to be very pleasant working here. The Margarita's got a pool and sunbathing areas, hasn't it?'

'Oh, yes, Roger,' Crista replied, a trifle sarcastically. 'It's got all the mod cons. At least for the time being, although just how much longer they're going to last for is quite another matter.'

'What do you mean?'

Crista hadn't really intended to tell Roger straightaway, but somehow, the words just spilled out of her, and she told him just how black the future looked for Eastwood Travel, although she omitted any mention of Hugo.

'So, what's going to happen?' he managed to say at last. 'Surely you can't expect me to get you out of this mess. Why didn't you tell me all about it when we talked on the phone? If you had then I wouldn't have . . . '

His voice trailed off lamely, but Crista felt certain that she knew what he was going to say. He wouldn't have come.

'Don't worry about it, Roger,' Crista said. 'It isn't your problem. I asked you to come out here, so why don't you just think of it as a free holiday?'

'That's a bit tough on me, isn't it? I was expecting to be part of the operation and make quite a bit of money out of all this, and now I find out that the company is virtually bankrupt.'

'It's hardly my fault,' Crista replied. 'I'd scarcely have wished it on my father's company. But is that the only reason you agreed to come out here, Roger? Because you thought you'd make lots of money? Why, you haven't even bothered to ask me how my father is.'

'I'm sorry, Crista. Of course that wasn't the only reason I came. I wanted to be of assistance to you. At the moment, I'm upset with the treatment I got at the airport. Hearing about Eastwood Travel was the last straw.'

'Then I won't bother you with any more details,' Crista replied sweetly.

9

Roger was quite happy to be dropped off at the Margarita, and made no plans to see Crista later that day.

'Don't worry about tonight,' he'd said, when she'd reluctantly suggested that he might want to have dinner with her. 'I'll still be tired. It'll probably take me the rest of the day to acclimatise. Besides, with all this trouble you've got, you'll have enough to do without worrying about me.'

And that was certainly true, Crista reflected, as she drove back to her apartment. She toyed with the idea of going back to the office, but what good would it do? Probably, she could call the company's lawyers or at least ask Stephen as Crista didn't actually know who they were, and ask them to do the necessary. But, somehow, she just couldn't bring herself to actually do the fateful deed. She was putting it off, and she knew it.

In the end, feeling fed-up and thoroughly sick of things in general, she changed into her bikini, put a towelling robe on, and decided to have a dip in the pool. Depositing her robe on a lounger, she dived straight into the pool, and swam briskly, finding that the exercise helped her fraught nerves. She didn't see Hugo approaching, and started violently when she heard him call her name.

'I'm sorry to disturb you, Crista, but I need to talk to you.'

She paused by the side of the pool.

'What do you want?' she asked, with a touch of impatience.

'We can't discuss it like this.'

'Very well, if you'll go and sit down, I'll be with you in a few minutes.'

Crista climbed out of the pool and hurriedly dried herself but Hugo wouldn't tell her what he wanted until they were safely ensconced in her apartment. Once there, though, he didn't beat about the bush.

'I've been to my solicitors and had the documents drawn up for the amalgamation of Eastwood and Voyager Travel.'

He laid a sheaf of papers down on the coffee table.

'My, but you haven't wasted any time.'

'You may wish to read them through to ensure that everything is in order before you sign.'

'You're very sure I will, aren't you?' she asked.

Hugo smiled sardonically.

'Of course I am. You don't really have any alternative, do you?'

Crista was annoyed, but tried not to show it.

'There's no need for me to read them. I realise that at the moment I've no alternative but for you to run the business, but I'm not prepared to sign anything legal until I see how things actually go. After all, who knows? It may just turn out that we can't actually work together.'

'You intend to take an active part then?'

'Of course. Otherwise, I'd be betraying my father's trust in me.'

He gave Crista a look of grudging admiration.

'I'll agree to your terms for a trial period. How does a fortnight sound?'

Crista was amazed that he'd agreed to her idea, albeit that it was for such a short time. But never mind that, it was a reprieve, and if her father rested and didn't excite himself unnecessarily, he might well be back at the helm by that time, and Eastwood Travel would be saved. She didn't even pause to wonder just how that miracle was going to occur with the closing order on the Argentina unlikely to be lifted for much, much longer.

'A fortnight will be quite acceptable,' Crista replied.

He stood up, scooping the papers back into his hands.

'Are you sure you don't want me to leave these with you so you can read through them?'

'No, I don't need to read them yet, but don't worry, I'll make sure I do, very thoroughly, before the fortnight is up.'

'Just as you wish,' he replied formally. 'Until tomorrow, then. I'll be at the Margarita office at eight-thirty, and I'd appreciate it if you'd be punctual!'

And with that parting shot, he headed for the door.

'Just a minute,' she called.

Hugo paused.

'Yes?'

'We'll be working as equals, since I am not your employee, and I want to set the record straight right now. You've been kind enough to offer to help us out, and I admit that you know a great deal more about the travel business than I do, but I don't intend to be dictated to.'

'I hope you're not trying to shirk,' he replied, irritating her.

'For your information, Hugo Santiago, I have to go to the hospital tomorrow morning and if they give the

OK, I'll be taking Dad to the Las Palomas convalescent home.'

'I apologise,' he said sincerely. 'Obviously I wouldn't expect you to be at work then. In fact, I might even come with you.'

'No thanks. I don't want Dad having another heart attack!'

To her surprise, Hugo laughed.

'Touché! All right, Crista, I'll go over the accounts with Stephen in the morning. I should imagine there's a good deal to sort out, and you can come in when you're ready to, after lunch. Give my best regards to your father.'

And then he was gone. And he hadn't mentioned Roger, hadn't even asked if he'd arrived in Gran Canaria.

The following day, Crista was at the hospital just before ten. She'd put a call through to Roger suggesting that she pick him up for lunch at one o'clock. Roger had been quite agreeable to the suggestion, saying that he'd welcome the opportunity to sunbathe and swim in the morning.

But what was she going to say to him at lunch time? She'd hinted that there might not be a job for him, because of the state of Eastwood Travel's finances, but she hadn't revealed that the real reason was Hugo. Still, what did it really matter? She now knew that she no longer cared for Roger. He was just an empty shell, and Crista realised that she needed a real man, a man like Hugo Santiago! If she could trust him, that is, but sometimes, Crista felt as if she'd be better off trusting a rattle-snake. What sane person would wish to amalgamate with a company as heavily in the red as Eastwood Travel? Hugo was a hard-headed businessman. It just didn't make sense.

She couldn't believe Stephen's suggestion that Hugo was in love with her. How could he possibly care for Crista when she was a living reminder of such a tragic past which he wanted to put behind him? Therefore, there must be something else in it for him, and Crista intended to find out just what that something was before she signed anything. She forced these troubled thoughts out of her mind. She didn't want to worry her father with business matters.

John Eastwood was sitting in the reception area, fully dressed, and with a suitcase beside him, when Crista walked into the hospital.

'It's taken you long enough to get here, girl!' he bellowed in welcome.

Crista bent down and kissed his cheek.

'Less of the lovey-dovey stuff!'

Crista just smiled.

'Thanks, Dad, for trusting me enough to sign any documents relating to the company. Mind you, I'll feel a lot happier when you're back at the helm.'

'That's because you're still a novice, but you'll learn. You're not John Eastwood's daughter for nothing!'

The convalescent home was beautiful, an eighteenth-century house with wooden balconies, surrounded by lush, green gardens, with a stream running through and a large, patio area with comfortable-looking sun-loungers. Even John Eastwood had to agree it was nice, although he was most definite that his stay there would be very brief.

Crista was pleased, however, to see him engaged in a lively conversation with a lady of similar age as she returned to her car and headed for the hotel. Well, at least she didn't have him to worry about for the time being! Roger, however, was an entirely different matter. Fortunately, it was possible to by-pass the office area of the Margarita, and Crista did just that, taking the elevator straight up to Roger's room. She tapped at the door, but there was no immediate answer, so she knocked louder.

'If you're looking for me,' a voice came from behind her, 'I'm here.'

Crista turned round. Roger, clad in brief, white shorts, and a black and white T-shirt, was just behind her. One look at his face told Crista that he was in a bad mood, and she wondered what could have happened now to upset him. A morning's sun-bathing should have been harmless enough.

'Hello, Roger, have you had a good morning?' Crista asked, although it was quite obvious that he hadn't.

'No, I have not! I was quite prepared to be friendly with Santiago, thanked him for rescuing you, and even invited him to join us for lunch. But Santiago made it patently clear to me that I'm not welcome here!' he exclaimed, peevishly, as he put his key in the lock and opened the door. 'You may as well sit out on the balcony. I'll need to shower and change before we go out. That is, if you have the time to spend on me. From what I can gather, you're much too busy toadying to your friend, Santiago!'

'Of course we'll have lunch,' Crista said quickly. 'As to my toadying as you put it, I've had no choice but to allow Hugo into the business. Money had to be found from somewhere.'

Roger's expression was singularly unpleasant, as he said, 'Oh, really? And just what are you doing to earn this money, eh, Crista?'

'How dare you!' she breathed. 'That is the way you'd think, isn't it? Because that's what you're like yourself.'

Roger was momentarily disconcerted, and Crista saw that her remark had hit home.

'I do care for you, Crista,' he said, in a milder tone. 'But you must see that all this has been a terrible shock for me. I'd always thought that Eastwood Travel was flourishing, that you were wealthy and . . . '

He broke off abruptly, realising what he'd been about to say.

'Never mind,' he continued, lamely. 'We can discuss things over lunch.'

Afterwards, Crista wondered why she hadn't just walked out there and then. Certainly, she'd felt like doing so. Probably it was because she felt guilty because she'd asked Roger to come to Gran Canaria.

The lunch was a total disaster.

Crista was horrified to see Hugo sitting at a corner table in the restaurant. What was he doing here? OK, so Roger had been foolish enough to invite him, but she certainly hadn't expected him to come! Hugo stood up as the waiter showed them to his table. He looked at his watch pointedly, before saying, 'I'm so glad you managed to make it, at last.'

Crista scowled. It was bad enough having to have lunch with a petulant Roger, but to have Hugo there as well, and a Hugo who was blaming her for being late, after the morning she'd had, was too much.

'I didn't realise you were joining us!' Her voice sounded decidedly irritated, as the waiter pulled out her chair for her and she sat down. Roger, however, despite his previous remarks about Hugo, seemed to be pleased to see him.

'So glad you could make it, old chap. It's nice for Crista and I to have company, especially as we may well all turn out to be business partners yet.'

Hugo gave him a withering look.

'I thought it might be advisable for me to get to know you a bit better.'

'Oh, why? Are you contemplating offering Roger a job after all?' Crista asked innocently.

She was quite sure that Hugo had absolutely no intention of doing so, and, quite frankly, she didn't blame him. It was becoming increasingly clear that Roger would make an abysmal worker. It was Roger who answered her.

'Surely that's up to you. The old boy must have seen to it that you've still got some say in the company. It's not totally bankrupt, is it?'

Crista rounded on Roger sharply.

'Why is it that every time you open your mouth I get the impression that all you're interested in is my bank account?'

Roger opened and shut his mouth like a floundering fish while Hugo gave a contemptuous laugh.

'Please, feel free to choose what you like off the menu, Roger. This is my treat.'

Roger was still angry with Crista and gave her a sullen scowl. He then proceeded to order the most expensive dishes on the menu, but still managed to find fault with most of what was served to him. After a couple of glasses of vintage wine, however, he mellowed.

'I'm not adverse to a position with Eastwood Travel. Crista's no doubt told you that I have a first class honour's degree, best student of the year, so it would need to be managerial position. Possibly some sort of partnership could be drawn up. I could have a percentage of profits, and a salary befitting my status, of course. I've no doubt at all that I'd be able to get things licked into shape pretty quickly.'

Crista groaned. This was Roger at his most objectionable. In fact, Roger seemed to be far worse than she'd remembered him.

'Roger, I don't think I should have

invited you out here. You're a novice in the travel business, and the state things are in, Eastwood needs a professional.'

In other words, a man like Hugo Santiago, even if she couldn't quite bring herself to actually speak the thought. Roger was immediately angry.

'If that's the case, you shouldn't have asked me. I wasn't at all sure whether to come anyway. As you've probably guessed, the girl who answered the phone to you wasn't a friend of a friend, she's a young lady whom I've been seeing, just as a friend, of course,' he added quickly, as Hugo shot him a steely look. 'Her father's the managing director of a large publishing company, and you know how I've always had aspirations to write. If you'd have made the position clear in the first place, I wouldn't have come, but you didn't, did you?'

He got no further, as Hugo leaned across the table and said, 'You're a contemptible louse! And I assure you that I personally intend to see to it that you're on the next plane back to Heathrow and out of Crista's life for good.'

Hugo hadn't even raised his voice, but Roger was spluttering indignantly, colour rushing into his face. Crista was embarrassed. They were attracting attention. Roger stood up, and looked at them both with loathing.

'I never want to see either of you again,' he exclaimed loudly, then turned on his heel and stormed out of the restaurant.

Crista went to get up and follow him, but Hugo put a hand on her arm.

'Let him go. Surely you can see him for the worthless money-grabber that he is! He's no good. You deserve better than that, Crista!'

'For your information, not that it's any of your business, I'm not in the slightest bit interested in Roger. I haven't been for a long time, but I do appreciate being allowed to handle my own business as I see fit without interference from you.'

'But how were you handling it, Crista? You hadn't got him to go home, at least I have.'

'I said he could stay on at the Margarita for a holiday and leave when he wanted to, seeing as I'd bothered bringing him out here in the first place.'

'Rubbish! You'll need the room for some of the tourists who were booked into the Argentina!'

His lips curved in a smile as he went on.

'There's no sentiment in business, you know!'

'Oh, you're absolutely impossible!' Crista exclaimed, but although she resented Hugo's interference, she couldn't help but smile herself.

10

The next couple of weeks were probably the worst Crista had ever spent in her entire life. Hugo proved to be a martinet work-wise. He was a perfectionist, and he expected everyone else to be the same, and Crista made mistakes. She couldn't help it; she hadn't had enough experience.

One morning, just after Crista had been congratulating herself on successfully getting one of the major tour operators which Eastwood Travel dealt with to accept a block booking for guests who had been due to stay in the Argentina to stay in the Hibiscus in Tenerife instead, Hugo burst into her office, his face furious.

'Just what do you think you're doing now?' he'd demanded, not even waiting for Gloria to leave the room. 'You've really done it this time. Don't you even bother to check your facts before you book hoards of people into a hotel which no longer exists?'

'What do you mean?' Crista asked, the colour draining from her face.

Gloria, smiling nervously, made a hasty exit from the room.

'This is what I mean!' he stormed, flinging some papers on to her desk.

Crista picked up the papers and hastily perused them. The Hibiscus had closed three months earlier for major structural alterations and wasn't due to re-open for another six months.

'I'm sorry, Hugo,' she began.

'Sorry!' he repeated. 'Tell me, what good is that now that the damage is done? Surely to goodness you should have thought to ring through to the hotel to check that a booking for such a large number of people, over several months, was all right. Now I'll have to try and get you out of this mess. Why don't you just go back to your apartment and sunbathe for the rest of the day and leave business matters to those who know?'

It was too much for Crista. In the ten days they'd worked together, Hugo had been finding fault with her. Some of it was justified, but she'd had enough. He was undermining her authority.

'The time for the agreement to be signed is nearly here, isn't it?'

'Yes, but what's that got to do with anything? It was a foregone conclusion that you'd have to sign it from the very start, but you insisted . . . '

'I'm not signing,' Crista interrupted him, coldly. 'I've decided that Eastwood Travel will have to go into liquidation, and unpleasant though it is, I'm going straight over to Dad to tell him what I've decided.'

'Crista, wait!' Hugo called urgently, as she pushed past him, and headed for the door, but Crista wasn't prepared to listen to him.

John Eastwood was all smiles when Crista located him sitting on a rustic, wooden seat, reading a newspaper, in the Las Palomas gardens.

'Crista! Good to see you! Well, girl, I've got some excellent news for you. I can leave this place whenever I like. In fact, they tell me I can start running the company again, as long as I take things easier. Mind you, it should all be a piece of cake now that Hugo and I have decided to amalgamate and . . . '

'What did you say?'

Crista sank down on a seat. Her father looked momentarily abashed.

'I know I'd given you leave to sign agreements girl, but I still left some things that I could sign, if and when I was feeling well enough. Hugo came here to see me yesterday and made me see what a stubborn old fool I'd been refusing to bury the hatchet for something that happened years ago. Actually, when I got talking to him, I found that he wasn't such a bad chap after all. He's go-ahead, and he's got guts, and that's what's needed in business today. The outcome was that he'll take over the day-to-day running of both companies, but I'll come in and do a bit of work, and be available on an advisory basis. It should work well. What do you say, girl?'

What did she say? Crista was furious! There was so much to say!

'Dad, you've sold us out!' she said at last.

'Sold us out? What on earth do you mean? It's an amalgamation, not a sell-out. Actually, we've come out of this little lot very well. You do realise what the only other alternatives would have been, don't you? Hugo would have taken over the company, bought us out. We'd have been so much in his debt, or, failing that, Eastwood Travel would have had to go into liquidation. I couldn't have stood that, not after all the hard work I've had.'

Crista managed the ghost of a smile.

'I'm very happy for you, Dad,' she said in a whisper.

'Well, you don't look it, girl. Something the matter with you?'

Crista gave a mirthless laugh. She

supposed that was one way of describing the fact that she was in love with Hugo Santiago, even though she found it very difficult to even like him! As for Hugo himself, obviously he couldn't stand the sight of her because she reminded him too much of Marianne, and, subsequently, of Robin's death. That was why he kept on being so rude to her.

'I'll pack your things for you, Dad. Seeing you're allowed to leave, I'm sure you'll want to get back to the Margarita just as soon as possible.'

That night, Crista told her father that she intended to return to England. They were sitting in the lounge of his suite of rooms in the Margarita.

'You intend to do what?' he exclaimed.

'To go back to London just as soon as I can arrange a flight,' Crista replied miserably.

What choice did she have? She couldn't keep seeing Hugo day in, day out, knowing that he hated her for the memories she awakened in him, putting up with his insults.

'Good grief, girl, surely you're not still hankering after that fancy boy.'

'Roger?'

Despite her unhappiness, Crista couldn't stop a little chuckle of laughter.

'Oh, no, Dad, I assure you I'm not.'

'Yet you invited him out here,' John Eastwood persisted, still not totally convinced. 'Stephen told me how Hugo sent him off with a flea in his ear!'

'Yes, I know that. Hugo had no right to interfere, and Stephen shouldn't go around repeating things which I tell him in confidence.'

'Hah!' her father cried, with grim satisfaction. 'So you are chasing after the fancy boy. I tell you, Crista, that fellow's no good. He'll . . . '

'I'm not in the slightest bit interested in Roger, Dad. I'm only sorry that I wasted so much time on him. No, that's not why I want to go back. When I came out here, I kept the flat on because I thought I might not be cut out for the tourism business, and that's just the trouble, I'm not. I miss writing and doing my illustrations.'

'But you could still do that out here, and just spend some time in the business. It'll be yours one of these days, or half yours,' he amended.

'I may come back,' Crista prevaricated. 'But at the moment, I feel as if I need to spend some time in London.'

And that was true, she had to. She had to get away from Hugo, had to stop seeing his face in her every waking thought.

John Eastwood sighed.

'Well, I can't say that I'm not disappointed, I am, but I'll not stand in your way if you're sure that's what you want.'

'Thank you, Dad,' Crista replied, dropping a kiss on the top of his head.

Crista flew back to London the following afternoon, after having elicited a promise from her father not to tell Hugo of her intentions until after she'd gone. He'd been a bit surprised by that, and she wondered if he suspected that she was actually running away from Hugo. He hadn't said as much, but, knowing him well, she had her suspicions.

Still, he'd kept his word, and for that she was grateful. But settling into life in London didn't prove to be as easy as she'd anticipated.

For one thing, her mind seemed to have a mental block. No matter how much she thought, she couldn't seem to come up with any fresh ideas, and even the illustrations she was producing were of very mediocre quality. She knew that her agent, Anne, was disappointed.

'Crista, what's wrong with you?' she'd asked, looking at one of Crista's poorer sketches with a look of dismay. 'You used to do far better work than this. What's the matter with you? Are you in love or something?'

Dispirited that day, Crista had gone back to her apartment. Perhaps she ought to look for a job. At least temporarily. It would take her mind off things, and, in time, she would hopefully be able to get back to her writing and illustrating.

She was sitting perusing the newspaper's jobs column one Friday evening, when the doorbell sounded. Crista started. She hadn't encouraged her friends since getting back. Most of them had been people Roger knew, so she hadn't really felt like cultivating them anyway.

Stealing a quick glance in the mirror, she pushed an errant strand of hair back from her forehead, and with the safety chain still in place, opened the door. Hugo Santiago, dark, handsome, and exotically out of place, was standing on the landing outside her door!

'Let me in, Crista, I have to talk to you, please,' he murmured, a curiously humble note in his voice.

Crista hesitated. There was nothing that she wanted to do more, but could she afford to take the chance of him hurting her still more?

'What do you want?' she asked hoarsely.

'Let me in, and I'll tell you. After all,

I've come a long way to see you.'

That was true. She owed it to him to hear him out.

'Very well, come in. Please sit down,' she said, indicating one of the aged, but comfortable, armchairs once she'd unlocked the chain.

'Would you like a drink, or some coffee?' she asked nervously.

It was so disconcerting having him sitting there, looking at her like that.

'Later,' he said, holding up a hand. 'For the moment, sit down, Crista, and talk to me. Don't be frightened, I won't bite.'

His smile was curiously endearing, and Crista found herself smiling with him as she sat down opposite him.

'First of all, I want to apologise for the way I treated you when we were working together. I realise now that I was unnecessarily hard on you, and I only hope that you can find it in your heart to forgive me. As I said to you before, superficially, you're very like Marianne. I've never forgiven her for what she did, and I never will. But where I made my big mistake was in trying to fight my growing love for you because you resemble her. I was afraid to let myself admit that I was falling in love with you because I was frightened that you'd hurt me the way she did.'

He gave a mirthless laugh.

'After Marianne, I swore to myself that I'd never let another woman get under my skin, and then you came along, John Eastwood's daughter, with a very distinct passing likeness to my ex-wife. I know it doesn't sound very admirable, but I thought that history was going to repeat itself.'

He passed a hand across his forehead, and gave Crista a tentative smile.

'I'm not putting this very well, am I? What I really mean to say is that I didn't want to fall in love with you, but being without you has made me realise in no uncertain manner that I have! Please say that you'll forgive me, Crista, my love.'

Crista hesitated, wondering if she

should put up some sort of a fight, some show of resistance. But then she smiled. What was the point? It would only be a pretence.

'I'll forgive you, Hugo. But you really mean that you're in love with me?'

Hugo was on his feet, covering the short distance between himself and Crista. Leaning down, he lifted her from her chair, and drew her into the warm circle of his arms.

'Of course I love you! Could you possibly love me?'

'I've loved you for quite a while, actually, Hugo, but that last fortnight you had me quite convinced that you positively hated the sight of me!'

'Oh, my love, my love!' he said, against her hair. 'I'm so very sorry, but I promise that I'll spend my life making it up to you, if you'll let me.' He looked anything but confident, as he added, 'You will marry me, won't you?'

'Yes, of course I will!'

Then she remembered her father,

remembered the emnity between the two men.

'But what will Dad say?'

'Don't worry, he knows why I've come to see you, and he's given me his blessing.'

'Then I see no impediment at all.'

Hugo was smiling as his lips claimed hers.

THE END

We do hope that you have enjoyed reading this large print book.

Did you know that all of our titles are available for purchase?

We publish a wide range of high quality large print books including:
Romances, Mysteries, Classics
General Fiction
Non Fiction and Westerns

Special interest titles available in large print are:
The Little Oxford Dictionary
Music Book, Song Book
Hymn Book, Service Book

Also available from us courtesy of Oxford University Press:
Young Readers' Dictionary
(large print edition)
Young Readers' Thesaurus
(large print edition)

For further information or a free brochure, please contact us at:
Ulverscroft Large Print Books Ltd.,
The Green, Bradgate Road, Anstey,
Leicester, LE7 7FU, England.
Tel: (00 44) **0116 236 4325**
Fax: (00 44) **0116 234 0205**

THE DOCTOR WAS A DOLL

Claire Vernon

Jackie runs a riding-school and, living happily with her father, feels no desire to get married. When Dr. Simon Hanson comes to the town, Jackie's friends try to matchmake, but he, like Jackie, wishes to remain single and they become good friends. When Jackie's father decides to remarry, she feels she is left all alone, not knowing the happiness that is waiting around the corner.